BOOK ONE

JACQUELINE FRIST

Archway Publishing books may be ordered through booksellers or by contacting:

Archway Publishing
1663 Liberty Drive
Bloomington, IN 47403
www.archwaypublishing.com
1 (888) 242-5904

ISBN: 978-1-4808-3144-5 (sc)
ISBN: 978-1-4808-3145-2 (hc)
ISBN: 978-1-4808-3146-9 (e)

Library of Congress Control Number: 2016909205

Print information available on the last page.

Archway Publishing rev. date: 9/14/2016

DEDICATION

To Miranda, who helped and encouraged me through the journey of writing this book.

I

Going to a doomed island in the middle of the ocean wasn't something I was planning to do that summer. I wouldn't have been on the stupid trip if it weren't for Terri, my twin sister. She just had to beg my mom to go somewhere exciting, so my mom dumped us there. She said our grandfather, Theodore Hunter III, owned a resort that was supposed to be loads of fun.

I didn't really know my grandfather. Every time I asked about what he did or any details about him, my mom just pretended she was busy, so I never learned much about him.

So Terri and I found ourselves on a boat headed to the island, about fifty miles off the coast of California. I liked to stand on deck and let the cool, gentle breezes weave through my hair, smell the salt air, and catch a whiff of fish while wondering what the island would be like.

Terri was jumping all around and asking a bunch of questions as she usually did. "How long till we get there? What's the island like? What's grandfather like? I can't wait to meet him!"

"I don't know," was all the patient captain would tell her.

I'd heard a few other kids were there also. I hoped that they were my age, fifteen or sixteen maybe, and that they wanted to hang out with me so I wouldn't be bored the whole summer. I'm one minute and twenty-four seconds older than Terri, so I was technically the older brother.

I also wondered what the island looked like. I imagined it as a luxurious paradise with butlers serving us strawberry-lemonade frozen drinks as we lounged. I conjured up visions of perfect beaches, soft and warm sand, and gentle breezes pushing small waves to shore.

I pictured a giant hotel with special rooms for Terri and me complete with snack bars, TVs, soft beds, and maybe a video game console. I figured chefs would prepare our meals and we could watch movies in a theater room while munching on candy bars and popcorn. I dreamed of the happiest place imaginable complete with helicopter service so I could go back to California for a day or so whenever I wanted.

"Jayce! Hello? Are you there? Jaaaaaaaayce! Are you daydreaming again?"

That was Terri.

"What? Oh, sorry. Quit yelling at me. I'm thinking."

"Whatcha thinkin' about?"

Sometimes, it seemed she just *wanted* to annoy me. "None of your business. What did you want to tell me?"

"It's lunchtime. Come in the cabin to eat. We're still fifteen miles away. We'll get there in about forty-five minutes."

"Fine. I'll be there in a few minutes."

Terri, being her usual vivacious self, skipped into the cabin. I realized my stomach was indeed growling. I hadn't eaten all day because I was afraid of getting seasick.

In the cabin, I saw a table with two chairs. Terri was in one, munching on a turkey-avocado sandwich. I always thought avocados were disgusting, but she loved them so much she'd have them as snacks by themselves. She was weird like that, but I was used to it. I sat, unwrapped my sandwich, and bit into it. Mine was roast beef with mayo, which I devoured. It tasted great. I wiped mayo off my mouth and took a sip of water.

Terri hopped outside to look at the seagulls; she hoped one would land on her arm for a bite of turkey. I asked the sailor how far we were from the island.

He smiled. "Really close." He pointed to a dim outline of an island on the horizon. "We're almost there."

I was relieved the boat trip was almost over. My stomach had started churning from the sandwich and the ship's rocking. I saw the island get bigger and bigger. Soon enough, we docked alongside at least ten other boats.

An old man who looked young for his age came up to us. "Jayce! Terri! Welcome to Blueview Island!" I was sure he was my grandfather Theodore.

2

Terri shouted, **"Granddad Theodore!"** even though she had never met him.

He was tall and had gray, curly hair. He had a cane but didn't seem to have any walking problems. He wore a suit; I guessed that was his work outfit. His voice sounded like a bass drum.

"Hello, Terri! Hi, Jayce. You guys can just call me Theo. I think Grandfather Theodore is too long and formal. Welcome to the island! I'm sure you'll get along well with the other workers here. Yes, you're going to work here, but don't worry, it'll be fun!"

I'm not too sure about that, I thought. I scanned the area, which was nothing like I had expected. I saw a big, open field in the middle of the island with a small, old hotel. No helicopters, no butlers with drinks on trays. I saw a volleyball pit and a pool, and the beach looked nice. I spotted a restaurant with a patio and some people inside eating lunch. Everything else seemed to be pretty much a massive, dense forest. I hoped I could live through the summer without dying from boredom.

"I'll show you guys to your room," Theo said.

He walked over to another building I hadn't seen yet that was bigger than the restaurant but not by much. Apparently, it was a shop. A sign read, "The Blueview Shop" in curly letters. *Yeah, really creative name.* "We're going to live ... in a shop?" I asked.

"Not necessarily," Theo explained. "Your rooms are *above* the shop."

He took us through the shop, which had lame Blueview T-shirts and merchandise that read, "It's the paradise getaway you've always dreamed of!" I quickly decided it wasn't. We went through an "Employees Only" door behind a rack of T-shirts with some fishing designs. We went up an old, wooden staircase and through a door that opened into a hallway with three more doors. Theo pointed to the nearest one. "See this door? This is *my* room. Never go into it. I forbid you." Terri and I nodded. The second door said, "Storage." The last door had a golden doorknob.

"Here we are," Theo announced, "the place you'll be staying for the next couple of months." He turned the knob. I hoped my room would be nice. I'd hoped too soon.

Terri and I went inside and saw nothing we had expected. We were obviously going to be sharing a room. Two beds were across from each other but not by much. The room was small. Everything was crammed together. The old carpet on the floor was more scruffy than soft. A rickety wooden chair and a small desk with a lamp sat in a corner. It looked like no one had sat there in a year. By the beds stood little shelves; the bottom shelf was just big enough for my suitcase.

A couple of skylights let in a little illumination but just

made the room look dull. Between the beds was a window that surprisingly offered a pretty good view of the forest. I could see the woods stretching all over the island to a tip occupied by a giant rock with a huge oak tree on top of it. *One day I'll have to go there.*

"All right, I'll leave you guys settle in. I'll be giving tours if you need me. The other kids, Zack and Emmett, are working right now, but Livia is somewhere around here. See you around!" Theo vacated the room.

"I'm so excited to meet the other guys here!" Terri said as she grunted and tossed her giant, purple, customized suitcase on her bed.

I slid my suitcase onto the lower shelf and plopped on my bed. I looked at the ceiling.

"Everyone knows doing nothing doesn't get you anywhere near having a fun time," said Terri, who was bouncing on her squeaky bed.

"Okay, we'll look around the island. Let me unpack first," I said, as I reached for my bag.

"Let's go now!" she said. She grabbed my arm and pulled me out the door.

"Okay, okay, okay. Fine. But once we're done, I'm coming back and unpacking. Nothing else."

"Deal," Terri said with a smile.

Man, I loved her dazzling smile. She'd gotten her braces out a few months before, so her teeth were straight, white, and pretty. I'd gotten mine out too, but my smile wasn't nearly as flattering as hers was. How could she be so perfect with that smile and her long, brown hair?

"Let's go!" Terri said, dragging me out the door.

I snapped to attention. "Okay, okay, fine! I'm coming!"

We went down the hallway and clomped down the creaky stairs. We walked around the shop, weaving our way through the merchandise to the door. We were going to see the island.

3

We walked across the field with all the buildings and stopped by a sign in the middle of the field that had arrows pointing different ways—"Blueview Shop", "Hiking Trail," "Beach," "Dock," "Blueview Hotel," and so on.

"Look at the top of the pole!" Terri said.

I looked up, shielding my eyes from the bright sun and saw a red bird in a nest. I'd never been interested in birds, so I didn't know what kind it was. It chirped at us, but its chirp was different from other birds'. This one seemed soothing, as if it had something magical about it.

"It's so pretty!" Terri said as she walked around the pole trying to get a better look at the bird.

It chirped at us a few more times before we headed toward the dirt trail that led through trees—massive giants staring down at those who dared go through. As we walked through, I pulled out my little notepad—I'd never told anyone but Terri I had it—and started writing and drawing in it. Terri was dragging behind taking her time to look at everything as she always did.

I was what I'd guessed to be halfway down the trail when I heard a voice from above that made me almost jump.

"Hey you!"

I shoved my notepad into my pocket. I looked up. "Who's there?"

A girl was swinging across the trees. She was beautiful and looked about my age. The girl had long reddish brown hair and amazingly blue eyes. She wore a necklace with a key attached. I saw her swing across the trees, making her way farther and farther down until she was a little higher than me but still in a tree. I could tell she liked to be up high.

"Hey, I'm Livia. Are you Jayce?" she asked, smiling.

"Yes. We were just looking around the island. I thought we were looking for you, but I guess you found us," I said, grinning.

"I was climbing my favorite tree, waiting for you to show up." She grabbed a branch, leaned to the left to look behind me, and pointed to Terri. "Is that Terri?"

"Yeah. She's a little too excited to be here."

Terri ran up to Livia. "Hi, I'm Terri! I'm guessing you're Livia. I bet we'll have so much fun on the island!"

"Excuse my sister's hyper state. She's always been a little wild."

Livia grabbed a branch, swung on it, and landed in front of me. She was just a touch shorter than me. "No problem! I like her excitement. It gets me fired up. It's almost dinnertime. Let's go to the restaurant! I'm starving. Since we work here, we always either get our food for free or half price."

"What's for dinner?" I asked.

"I don't know. Let's go find out. I'm so hungry I could eat a cow." She smiled.

We walked back the way we had come. Livia and I were walking together; Terri was behind us because the trail was too narrow for all three of us.

"I was thinking about building a tree house or something in that tree," Livia said, pointing. "You want to help? It could be our summer project!" she said and nudged me.

I hadn't climbed a tree in a while, but I wasn't scared of heights. I said, "Sure, it'll be fun." Then I lowered my voice. "But you might not want to ask Terri. She *hates* heights."

"That's okay," Livia said. "So does Zack. And Emmett isn't really the build-and-climb type. So it can be just our thing."

Our thing. That sounded as if we'd been friends forever even though I'd known her for only a few minutes. Man, she was friendly. Terri and I had been on the island for only a few hours, but I'd already made good friends with a girl who liked what I liked to do.

Once out of the woods, we headed to the restaurant. Livia checked her phone. "Shoot. Gotta go. I'll see you guys tomorrow. Theo gave Zack, Emmett, and me a day off so we could hang out with you guys. See you guys!" She ran toward the hotel, and I could've sworn she winked at me.

The rest of the day, we ate some extra sandwiches from the boat and walked past the pool, volleyball court, beach, and so much more that by the time I was in our room unpacking, I was exhausted.

I put my clothes in one of the two tiny closets in our room and plopped onto my bed. Though the mattress was old, it was soft, so I knocked off right away.

4

The next day, Livia introduced us to Emmett, a boy with chocolate-brown hair and blue eyes, and Zack, a tough, buff-looking guy with olive skin. He looked like he'd be happy to sucker-punch someone any minute.

"Jayce, Terri, meet Zack and Emmett," Livia said.

"Hey, guys, I'm Emmett, Emmett Newman," the boy said with a grin.

"Hello, I'm Zack McCarthy," Zack said and smiled. His voice was deep, a bit lower than mine. It reminded me of my dad's voice or at least what I'd been told he sounded like. I suddenly felt my stomach wrench, but I quickly pushed the thought away and said hi to Zack and Emmett.

They showed us around the island more, and we learned about a climbing wall on the cliff side and a campsite on the other side of the island. As we were walking on the trail to the site, Zack walked toward me and said in a low voice, "Hey dude."

"Yeah?"

"I ... I think I have a crush on your sister. She's nice, funny, and cute too. I like her already."

I smiled. "Dude!" I pushed him playfully so he'd know I was fine with it.

We got to the campsite, a huge, open area with a big firepit in the middle. I saw a few tents around it and some families walking around and doing camp-like stuff. I planned on camping there one day, maybe with all my new friends.

As we were walking toward the climbing wall, I saw Zack talking to Terri, who was flirting with him. That wasn't surprising. I figured she probably had a crush on him too; she was laughing at everything he said. I guessed they were perfect for each other.

Livia showed us the climbing wall, which was awesome, and after lunch, we decided to play volleyball—guys against girls. Terri, being a volleyball nut, was the best of the girls, but Livia was pretty good too, and Emmett was the best out of all the guys. Zack and I weren't very good, but we had fun. We played for hours, and of course the girls won every time.

Theo stopped by to see how we were doing, and he told Emmett he had to work.

"Aww, dang. See you guys at dinner!" He walked off with my grandfather.

We said good-bye to him and resumed the game, but it wasn't as fun since Emmett had been our key player; Zack and I stunk by ourselves.

When the sun started to set, we headed to the restaurant. On the way, Zack stopped Terri and whispered something to her. She smiled and whispered something back.

"You guys go ahead," Zack said. "I want to show Terri something. We'll catch up later."

Livia shrugged as if she didn't care. I didn't either, so I said, "Okay. Have fun."

Livia told them, "You might miss out on the special! We'll eat all your food." She smirked.

Zack and Terri scurried off as Livia and I turned toward the restaurant. "So, uh, what do you guys do for fun out here besides climbing and building?" I asked.

"I mainly spend my time in the woods or on the trail, but Zack and Emmett like to go to the beach and play volleyball there or go to the pool. Sometimes, they watch movies in their rooms or play a game in the field."

"I can tell Terri will be with them a lot since she's not the adventurous type. I'm that kind of person, though," I said.

"Then we'll get along great."

"What's your favorite thing about nature and the forest here?" I asked, trying to keep the conversation from becoming awkward.

"Probably the trees. It's amazing how tall they grow. What about you?"

"I'd say the squirrels, but I'm not sure why. I think it's cool how they can hang onto trees and climb so high without falling."

"Well, Squirrel Boy, you hungry? Let's hope the special tonight is not squirrel meat." She laughed. I liked her laugh. It made me smile and feel happy.

"Okay, I'm fine with that, Tree Girl." I was grinning like an idiot.

"Whatever, Leaf Head."

"Nature Girl."

"Branch Boy."

We laughed at our inventiveness with names.

We saw Emmett, who looked confused and pointed behind us. "Where are Zack and Terri going?"

"We don't know. They said they'd be back later," I said.

"Well," Livia said, "Let's eat. I'm starving."

The restaurant looked interesting from the outside. It was surrounded on three sides by glass, so diners could look out at the surroundings. The redbrick wall on the fourth side was where the kitchen was. The patio was dotted with red tables and chairs each with huge, red umbrellas. I guessed the restaurant manager must have liked red a bunch.

We entered through glass doors, and I was so busy looking around that I almost ran into Emmett. Blueview Island merchandise was hanging on the walls along with some camping items, fishing rods, canoe paddles, and even some fish hanging from ceiling, which was pretty high up there. Baskets of plastic forks, knives, spoons, and napkins rested on the tables, which were numerous.

People were placing their orders at a counter. We went there, where an adult was working. Above us were chalkboards that announced the menu. One sign read, "Sunny Beachside Restaurant Special: Large Pizza with your choice of toppings, half off!" with a picture of a pizza.

"You guys want to share a pizza?" I asked.

"Sure," Emmett said.

"No thanks," Livia said. "I don't like pizza very much."

I stared at her. "How do you *not* like pizza?"

"I just don't," Livia said, starting to get interested in her shoes. She looked up. "I'm just going to get the fish."

Emmett and I ordered a large pizza with pepperoni

and sausage, and Livia ordered trout. I had no idea how she could eat that stuff; I thought it was disgusting.

We took a table and set up the number the guy at the counter had given us. We made sure we left room for Zack and Terri. Livia and I sat next to each other; Emmett sat two seats away. I guessed he wanted to sit next to Zack.

"So what are you guys doing later tonight?" Livia said while twirling a plastic fork.

"Probably sleep," I said.

Emmett looked at me funny. "That's it? That's all you're gonna do?"

"Um, yeah, I think so."

Livia put down her fork. "Dude, here on the island, we don't just 'go to bed' after dinner. We have fun. Lots of it."

"All right, what are you guys going to do?"

They smiled. "You'll see," Emmett said, "but if you're gonna hang out with someone at night, you'll want to hang out with Livia. She does the kinds of things I think you'll like."

"All right," I said. I turned to Livia. "I'll come with you after dinner. But it better be fun." I smiled, and she smiled right back. Then she looked behind me.

I turned and saw Zack and Terri walking through the doors laughing. They spotted us, came over, and sat.

"He showed me some special spots around the island. It's so pretty!" Terri said, smiling at Zack. Their eyes met. I could sense they'd established a connection.

"Glad you guys had fun because there's going to be even more tonight!" Livia said, giving me a smile.

A waitress came over with our pizza. The aroma filled our noses. She put a fish dish in front of Livia. The smell wasn't as appealing, but she seemed to relish it, so I didn't say anything.

"Yummy! Pizza," Terri said, reaching for a piece.

I grabbed the biggest slice I could and put it on my plate. I raised it, felt the hot steam flow onto my face, and took a huge bite. My taste buds started dancing. The cheesy, gooey, savory taste bounced around in my mouth. It was the best pizza I'd ever had. I wanted to eat at the restaurant all the time. I finished my slice and helped myself to another. I could've eaten the stuff for days. It was so good, and by the huge smile on Terri's face, I saw she really liked it too. One slice remained on the pan, and for a moment, we all looked at it and at each other. We knew we all wanted it.

"I'm full," said Emmett, who had three pieces of crust on his plate.

"You guys can have it. I probably shouldn't eat any more," Terri said.

Zack and I looked at each other. We smiled and were about to snatch the piece, but I had an idea. I felt for my lucky quarter in my pocket, pulled it out, and showed it to Zack. "Heads or tails?"

"Heads."

I flicked the coin way up, praying for tails. It did about a dozen flips before landing in my palm. I smacked my palm on top of my other hand and looked at Zack before lifting my hand. He smiled and nodded. I raised my hand. Tails. I laughed. "I won! Better luck next time." I thanked my lucky quarter as I ate the slice. I almost always won with that coin.

"All right, you won, dude, but next time, we're competing in a different way," Zack said.

Livia had finished her meal and seemed satisfied. "Do you want to go outside now?"

"Yeah, let's go," Livia said. "I always need to move around after I eat, so let's have some fun."

We got up and wound our way through the tables to the door.

"Are we going to see the others later tonight?" I asked.

"Yeah, probably. Tomorrow night's campfire night. We have a bonfire on the beach. They'll be there, so we can spend time with them tomorrow."

"Do you guys have it every week?"

"Two to three times a week. I think you'll like it."

I followed Livia to the edge of the forest, but we didn't go in. "What are we doing?" I asked.

"Hold on. Stay here."

She walked to a shed nearby that sported a sign: "Authorized Personnel Only." She disappeared inside for a few seconds and popped back out with many items: a plastic bag, some black clothing, two hats, two jackets, and some weird-looking metal things attached to a long rope with knots every foot or so on it.

"What the heck?" I said.

"Put these on." She tossed me a black hat and coat.

"What are we gonna do, rob a bank?" I said with a laugh.

"No, but it'll be fun," she said as she donned her jacket.

I put on the hat and jacket and followed her into the woods to a massive tree not far from the one she'd been in when I met her.

She put down her gear and handed me one of the metal things. It had two wheels inside, like pulleys. The rope dangled from it. I tried to figure out what we were doing.

After she got her gear situated, she started climbing the tree. I looked up. The tree had so many branches big and small that I couldn't see what was at the top, but I had a feeling there was something up there.

"Follow me," Livia said. "You're gonna like this." We started our journey up.

5

It was tough climbing mainly because the rope and the metal contraption were getting heavy. I followed her. We grabbed branches and made our way higher and higher. We nearly reached the top; we stood on a branch huge enough to support us.

"What are the black clothes for?" I asked.

"So no one sees us, finds us, or knows who we are. Theo doesn't like kids in the forest at night, so just blend in with the darkness. We'll be fine." Livia started walking down the branch toward a wire attached to the tree. I knew exactly what we were going to do.

"No way! A zipline? I've always wanted to try one!" I exclaimed.

"Well, now's your chance. I built this a while ago, and most nights, I come here and do this. Come on! There are five ziplines and a surprise at the end. Hang on because it's a little dangerous."

She put down the plastic bag.

"What's in the bag?"

She paused. "None of your concern. One of my projects."

Before I could reply, she put her metal pulley on the wire, held onto the rope, put her feet into a loop in the rope, and zipped off into the dark trees with a whizzing noise. The noise faded and stopped.

Silence. Then I heard, "It's clear! You can come now!"

I had a little trouble getting the metal thing hooked up to the wire, but when I thought I had it on right, I tried to do what Livia did. I was trying to go slowly so I wouldn't fall, but as soon as my feet went off the branch I became a bullet.

I flew through the trees. A few leaves smacked me in the face, but I didn't care. I felt the cool wind blow my hair around. I felt flying was actually possible. I was breaking the laws of nature. I saw the ground far below, but I wasn't scared. I was laughing and having so much fun. I saw a small platform ahead of me on which Livia was standing and smiling.

I angled my feet forward and landed on the platform, but I was a little clumsy with my touchdown. I staggered a little, but I regained my balance and stood.

"Like it?" Livia asked.

"I haven't had that much fun in months!" I exclaimed as I got my rope off.

"Good!" Livia said. She peered through some trees. Suddenly, she grabbed my hand and pulled me down low on the platform. "Stay down. Be quiet!"

I was about to say, "Hey! What are you doing?" but I saw the beam of a flashlight.

"Every night, Theo sends some workers out to make sure no kids are on the trail or in the trees. He doesn't mind people doing night runs, but if they find us, we'll never get to do this again," Livia whispered. She looked down, realized she was still holding my hand, and let it go. She watched the figures with flashlights.

They walked the trail, waving their flashlights all around. When a beam of light got near us, we shrunk as low as we could. Our black hoods kept them from spotting us. They walked down the trail. Livia waited until the beams of light faded so much that we couldn't see them anymore.

Livia smiled. "They never find me. They never will."

I laughed. "That makes you sound like a criminal."

"Well maybe I am, maybe I'm not. Come on, we still got another four lines."

"Aw man, only four?"

"Well, they're really long, and we can do this whenever we want. You live here now, remember?"

"Oh yeah." I smiled. The whole situation made me so happy. I'd gotten there just a few days ago, and the place wasn't bad, the people were so much fun, and I liked Livia a bunch. She was the kind of girl who didn't stay home and watch TV or go on her phone; she obviously liked the outdoors, like me. I thought the summer wouldn't be so bad after all.

Livia asked if I wanted to go first on the next zipline. I did exactly what I'd done to get on the first one, but that time, I went backward. I smiled at her, she giggled, and I whizzed off.

We went through all the ziplines and were on the last platform. "How do we get down?" I asked, looking for a ladder.

"There's a thick rope over there. We'll slide down it,"

Livia said. "But wait, I want to show you something," she said, pulling her pulley off the wire. "Take off your black clothing and follow me."

She took off her black clothes and started to climb up a few branches, and I followed her. We went up and sat on some big branches at the top of the tree, and the area had no branches in the way, so we could see the sky perfectly. It was really dark. The stars were on display for us.

"Wow! How come I never see this many stars at night anywhere else?" I asked.

"Because most places have too many lights, but not the forest. There's just us," Livia said. Just for a moment, our eyes met. She turned and looked at the stars.

I sat next to her. For a while, all was silence except for the crickets. Moonlight illuminated the area around us.

After a while, she asked, "Did you ever like a girl in California?"

"What do you mean 'like'?"

"I mean a girl you really liked and you had a crush on her." Livia turned to me, waiting for an answer.

"Not really. There was one girl who was a good friend, but I didn't have a crush on her, so I don't think that counts. What about you?" My heart hurt for a second at the reminder of leaving my friends, including her.

"Once, but it's been awhile since I moved here, and I haven't seen him in forever, so I don't like him that much anymore. I don't know if he has a girlfriend or not since we haven't talked in forever."

"If you've been here for a while, what about your parents? Wouldn't you want to visit them? Or do they work here?" I asked, trying to change the subject. I felt uncomfortable talking about my crush with a girl.

Livia was silent. I waited for a response. She finally sighed. "Well, I've never liked my dad. He was so mean to my mom and me. He was terrible to my mother. Once, when I was younger, they were arguing about something, I didn't know what, but he was so angry that he started hitting my mom. I ran in to stop him, but he smacked me, which I haven't forgiven him for. I've hated him ever since. So my mom divorced him. We moved away so I barely see him anymore. I don't mind, though. When I do see him, he's always with his new wife and their two sons. He hides the secrets about what he did to us so they don't think he's bad. The two boys, Jackson and Tyrone, bully me, while my dad and his new wife treat me like I'm unwanted. I don't like to think of him as my dad.

"As for my mom, a couple of months later, she started going out to bars more often, and she stayed out late. When she came home, she always went straight to bed. I started seeing her less and less. She'd look for jobs all day every day, but she never found one. I had to start working for the people in our neighborhood so I could make some money for us.

"One night, about a year after the divorce, she was driving drunk and crashed into a car. She still has a lot to pay for the damage to both cars, the hospital bills, and for driving drunk in the first place. She went into an even steeper spiral after that. I decided she was no longer my mother but instead a raging alcoholic, so I came here to get away from my terrible life at home. I can take care of myself here." Livia sighed again and looked at the stars. The night fell silent.

I felt like I needed to say something. "I'm so sorry to hear all that." I decided I really liked her. She trusted me and was very nice to me. It seemed as if we had a special connection. "I thought this summer was going to be terrible," I said. I hesitated. "But now that I know you, this will be the best summer ever." I did something I'd never done before. I took her hand in mine.

She looked at me, but she didn't look agitated, or angry, or surprised. She smiled. I smiled back. We looked up at the stars. It was so quiet and peaceful. While I was looking up, she leaned over and kissed me on the cheek. I knew, I completely knew as she rested her head on my shoulder that it was my best night ever.

6

The following night, I was excited for the camp-
fire. The others had already gone down to the beach, but
Livia wanted to show me where she had envisioned the
tree house being. After a while, she looked at her watch.
"It's time for the campfire. Wanna go?"

"I'd love to." I took her hand, and we started walking
toward the beach but at a nice, slow pace. We heard only
crickets and trees swaying in the breeze.

When we neared the beach, we saw an orange and
yellow glow getting brighter the nearer we got to it. We
heard voices, laughter, and a guitar playing softly. We
took some steps down from the dock to the beach and saw
Emmett, Zack, and Terri talking and laughing by a giant
fire. They saw us and waved. I noticed Zack had his arm
around Terri.

Everyone was sitting on logs that ringed the fire. I
saw the guitar player and a few people singing along. The
sound of the waves lapping the shore was soothing. The
fire illuminated the whole scene. I looked out to the sea
and saw the bright moon right above the horizon and
shining straight across the dark-blue water.

"It's about time you came," Terri said with a smile.

We walked to a table behind the guitarist and found supplies for s'mores. We grabbed sticks, and Zack, Emmett, and I fenced with them for a bit before joining the girls at the fire. Everyone had a marshmallow except Zack, who had two.

"Why don't you just cook them one at a time? Wouldn't one get cold while you eat the other?" I asked him.

"No, because one s'more wouldn't be as good without two marshmallows, duh," Zack said, smiling.

"How do you guys like your marshmallows cooked?" Terri asked, hovering her stick right above the flames.

"Golden-brown," Emmett said.

"Burned," Zack and I said in unison.

"Gooey but not burned," Livia said, looking in the fire.

"I'm with Emmett. Golden-brown," Terri said.

I caught mine on fire three times, as usual, and when I lifted my stick to blow out the flames, my marshmallow slid off into the fire. Emmett and Zack laughed, I guessed because it was funny or because of my weird expression. Livia giggled at my misfortune while Terri laughed her head off. She laughed hard even at the littlest things. I joined in the laughter as my marshmallow went up in flames.

I went back to the table for a new marshmallow, and I thought I saw a dark figure some ways off, where the water and sand met. I couldn't tell, but it seemed as if he was looking at the group around the campfire or even just at me. I figured it was someone who had broken away from the group to take a walk on the beach. I grabbed a marshmallow and went back to the blaze.

When our marshmallows were done, we went to the table to complete our s'mores. I grabbed a piece of chocolate and some graham crackers, but Zack stopped me. "Dude, no. Do it like this." He grabbed doubles of everything and made a stack of a graham cracker, chocolate, then a marshmallow, another chocolate piece, marshmallow, chocolate, then a graham cracker to top it all off.

"That's one huge s'more," I said. I laughed, wondering how he'd eat it. The girls were laughing hysterically as he tried to fit it in his mouth. I took the first bite of mine and thought the island felt more like home than any other place did.

I spotted the dark figure again, but in a different place. I knew it wasn't my imagination. He was just standing there ...

"Dude, what are you doing? Come on, wanna wrestle?" Emmett asked, giving me a playful punch.

I pointed at the dark figure. "You see that?"

"See what? I just see darkness," Emmett said, squinting.

"That dark figure there by the water."

"What? Oh yeah. Now I see. What about it?"

I wanted to say, "I don't know. It just seems ... weird," but it was hard to explain how I felt about the strange figure. It was as if I were connected to this person somehow or had seen him before though all I saw was a shadow.

Emmett looked at me as if I were being weird and laughed. "Man, you shouldn't worry about someone on the beach. He's probably just enjoying it. Come on, dude, I'm gonna tackle Zack."

I watched as he snuck up on Zack as he was talking to Terri and jumped on him, surprising his prey. All I saw after that was a tangled mess of arms and legs and sand flying everywhere as they tried to pin each other.

I laughed as Zack tried to pin Emmett who was a lot smaller. Emmett must have seen it coming, because he quickly shoved Zack off, rolled away, and jumped up quicker than Zack could realize he was flat on the sand.

Emmett helped him up, and they laughed and high-fived each other.

I felt a chill run up my spine even though I was next to the fire. My eyes darted to the spot where I'd first seen the shadow. It wasn't there. I walked to Livia and Terri, who were laughing about something, and asked, "Hey guys, um, have you seen anybody come into the crowd from that direction?" I pointed over their shoulders, and they turned to look.

"No, why?" Terri asked.

"Just curious. I think I saw someone over there, but now he's gone, so I didn't know if he came back to the fire or not." I was uneasy about the emptiness of the area where the figure had stood.

We walked back and stayed by the fire a little longer, joking around, laughing and talking as if we'd been friends forever. We headed back to the shop, and as Emmett, Zack, and Livia started heading toward the hotel, I said, "Livia! Wait!"

Emmett and Zack looked back but kept walking and playfully shoving each other. Livia stopped and turned around. "Yeah?"

I ran up to her. "Thanks for ... everything. I feel I've been friends with all you guys forever, and this place feels like home. I'm glad you showed me the ziplines last night and this beautiful island. You made this the time of my life." I wrapped my arms around her, and she did the same to me. I didn't want the night to end. I didn't want to move a muscle. I didn't want to leave Livia. It felt like the whole world stopped around us. Then she let go, and so did I but reluctantly. She said, "Goodnight" and started to jog to the hotel.

"Goodnight," I said and headed inside.

Terri was ready for bed when I got to our room. She was sitting up in her bed reading her favorite book for the tenth time. I got into a T-shirt and shorts for bed and went into our small bathroom. I could already tell Terri, the human tornado, had been in there; she was so much messier than I ever was. I wished for a different room or at least a different bathroom. Toothbrushes and toothpaste and hairbrushes were everywhere. I tried to get ready without getting the bathroom messier than it already was. I got in bed, stared at the ceiling, and reflected on my great day.

"So how was your day, sis?" I asked, hands under my head.

"Great! How is Livia so far?" she asked as she got under the covers.

"Amazing. You have no idea," I said. "Goodnight, Terri."

"Goodnight, Jayce."

I turned off my lamp. I didn't realize I was so tired. I fell asleep right when my head hit the pillow.

7

I had a crazy dream, a nightmare like none I'd ever had.

In it, Terri and I were little, no more than eight, but it seemed my usual, fifteen-year-old self was inside a little version of me. It seemed I was watching a movie but one from my own point of view. We were at our pool, the one at the house we lived in back then, and we were so excited about jumping in.

Being the obedient kid I was, I had put on sunblock and was wearing my goggles.

Terri said, "Jayce, wanna jump in together?"

"Sure! Ready? One, two, three!"

We both jumped as high as we could and plunged into the cool water. The whole world started to spin and shake as I did flips and turns in the water.

I looked around underwater to see Terri but couldn't spot her anywhere.

Suddenly, the pool got darker. It was as if I were in a pool of oil. I couldn't see anything. I didn't have much air left. I started to freak out. Voices came out of nowhere, whispering to me, "He's a liar, a liar!" "You'll regret what you have done." "Leave now before you die." "We know why you came."

I wanted to scream, to shout at the voices to go away, but I couldn't move or speak. I tried to swim up, but I didn't know what was up or down. Eventually, I figured it out and started to swim up and get help. I wondered if Terri was okay.

The voices continued. "You need to stop." "You don't know what you've done." "You changed everything."

I was almost to the surface. I reached up, and just before my hand broke the surface, I saw the same shadowy figure I'd seen on the beach just above the surface. Before I could catch a breath, it felt like the voices were grabbing my ankles and feet. I was about to explode from no air. They started pulling me down. I sank lower and lower, so I started thrashing and twisting.

"You shouldn't have come here." "For every action there's a reaction." "You don't know what you've done."

I was dragged down lower and lower. The harder I struggled, the more they pulled me down. Dark claws grasped my feet and dug into my skin. *Can't breathe! Can't breathe ... Need ... air ...*

For some reason, I could hold my breath longer than usual, but I knew I wouldn't be able to hold out much longer.

"You need to fix this."

I felt I was losing my sanity.

Don't breathe in! Don't breathe in!

Even my vision was fading. My brain hurt from the pressure. *Could this be possible even in a dream? Kick them! Just try!* Before I could, I blacked out.

8

When I woke up the next morning, I was in a cold sweat. I almost screamed when my eyes flew open. Terri was asleep. I decided to take time to think about my weird dream before telling anyone about it. I donned a T-shirt, sneakers, and shorts. I decided to take a hike and check out the hill, the one Emmett had told me was called Moonlit Hill since it was the only place fully covered with moonlight at night.

It was early in the morning. I walked quietly past Theo's door. I woke up early all the time, so I was used to being careful not to wake people up.

It was a humid day. The sun was just rising from behind the forest, so I knew it was sometime after six. I ran across the open field and down the gravel path to the hiking trail. I saw only a few people walking about. I knew the shops would open and the activities would start later. I ran to path that led through the monstrous trees and ran under the big sign, "Blueview Hiking Trail," into the woods.

As I ran, I listened to the birds. I saw a flash of red that startled me. The red bird I'd seen on the post the day before landed on a branch a little in front of me. It chirped at me, looking straight into my eyes. There was that chirp again, that weird, soothing sound.

I was curious. I raised my hand toward the branch, which was higher than I could reach, but I still got close to the bird. Instead of flying away, it jumped on my hand.

Surprised, I leapt back and almost fell, but the red bird stayed on my hand. It seemed unafraid, comfortable with me as if it knew me.

I continued my walk. The bird clung to my finger. I wondered why this bird was different. It twisted and turned its head, looking at me and then at the path ahead. It chirped at me. It cocked his head to the side while looking at me and jumped off my finger, flying away. It landed on a branch a little ways off the trail. It seemed to be trying to lead me somewhere.

There were many signs up and down the trail saying "Stay on the Path! Protect Your Environment!" but I was pretty far into the forest, and no one was on the trail but me, so I decided to follow the bird. I started running through leaves and sticks, avoiding thorns and jumping over sharp rocks.

As I neared the little red bird, I reached up, expecting it to jump on my finger again. But before it could, something under a thorn bush caught my eye. It shimmered and glistened in the sun. The bird stared at it, then glanced at me and chirped. I tried to pull apart the branches of the bush, but thorns cut my hand. I yelped when I saw a deep cut across my palm.

I got a few leaves to stanch the blood a bit. When the bleeding calmed down a little, I resumed my digging through the thorn bush but much more carefully.

Jacqueline Frist

Once I got past the thorns, I grabbed whatever it was, stood, and winced at my hurt hand. It was an oval metal thing with a hole in the middle. It was silver; I knew that because I used to be interested in metals and rocks. Other than a few thin, intricate, fancy designs on its edges, it was plain. On one side were small letters spelling *aegris*.

I turned it over and over but found nothing other than the designs; no indication of the maker or owner. It was about the size of a golf ball but oval. I messed around with it a little longer but couldn't figure out its purpose. I looked at the bird with a confused face and pointed to it. The bird chirped and flew to a closer branch for a better look at the silver object.

Curious, I looked through the hole and nearly fainted at what I saw.

9

Everything I saw through the hole was black and white. Dull. Dead. The trees had shriveled leaves and dead branches. Rocks were crumbled. The sky was dark. It was the most horrible sight I'd ever seen. I looked around through the little hole in the silver object. Everything looked dreary, terrible.

But when I spotted the little red bird through the hole, it was still ... red. It was the only thing with color in sight through the hole. It flew to a different branch. It chirped its familiar chirp, but it seemed to be trying to tell me something. I realized neither the bird nor the aegris thing was normal. I was overwhelmed. *How is this possible?*

Frightened but excited, I shoved the aegris into my pocket, got back on the trail, and ran as fast as I could to the field. I ran like a madman even after hearing Zack yelling at me in the distance. I decided I wasn't going to show him my find just then. *He shouldn't be the first to know.*

I sprinted to the shop, shot up the stairs, and broke into my room, where Terri was just getting out of bed.

"Terri! There's something I need to show you!" I almost

shouted, still baffled by the weirdness of a seemingly ordinary ring.

She looked tired and completely uninterested in what I had to say. "Ugh, now? I just got out of bed."

"You're gonna want to see this," I said, pulling out the silver object.

"What's that?" Terri asked, rubbing her eyes, unamused.

Just to make sure it still worked and I wasn't crazy, I looked through the hole again. Things were so different. The wood walls were rotted, our beds were crumbled up and covered in mold, and the carpet was shriveled up and burned.

Terri looked the worst of all. She had no eyes, skin that looked like rotting apple peels, and burned hair. She looked like a zombie but worse than I'd ever imagined one. I almost gagged.

"Well? What is that thing?" Terri asked, getting impatient.

"I woke up early, so I decided to hike in the woods and explore the island. I saw that red bird we'd seen, and it flew to me and landed on my hand. After a while, it flew to a branch off the trail, so I went toward it, and this thing caught my eye, and well ... it has some kind of special power."

Terri was confused but unamused. "What do you mean? It's just some stupid big ring."

"No it's not. When I look through it, everything looks, well, dead. And dull. Black and white and grey. Except when I looked at the bird. It was still a vivid red and alive." I waited for her response.

"Let me see that. Jayce, this is ridiculous. Stop trying to make the summer more interesting than it already is. Let me see it." Terri snatched the aegris from me and looked through the hole. She screamed, dropped the object and backed away. "What ... is ... that ... thing?"

"Calm down! It won't hurt you, I think. It's just weird." I picked it up. Surprisingly, it had no dents or scratches. "Be careful with it. I don't want it to lose its power or break."

Terri was frightened. "I'm not touching that thing *again!* Everything was gross, and scary, and—"

"Okay, fine! You don't have to look through it again, but I'm keeping it because I think it's gonna be useful. Why do you think the bird had color and looked alive but nothing else did?" I asked, trying to calm her down.

"I don't know! It's call sounded really weird. Maybe it spots unusual or strange things? Maybe even things that aren't normal," Terri said, still wary about the mystifying silver ring.

"Yeah, that must be it. The bird isn't normal. It *showed* me where to find this, and it was in color. Thanks, Terri!" I was excited about this amazing ring, weird as it was.

Someone knocked on our door. "Come in!" I said. The door opened slightly, and Zack poked his head in.

"Hey guys," Zack said. He smiled at Terri, and she smiled back. "I saw you sprinting across the field. Didn't you hear me yelling?"

"Uh, yeah. It's just that I really wanted to show Terri something."

"What did you show her?"

I could tell he was curious.

"This." I showed him the object. "If you look through it—"

Terri broke in. "It makes everything look dead and dull and—"

"Whoa, dudes, slow down," Zack said, eyeing the object.

"Well," I said. I hesitated. I glanced at Terri. She nodded as if to say *go on*. "It, uh, has some kind of power. If you look through this hole, it makes everything look dead and dreary. Except for things that aren't normal, which I know because I looked at an unusual bird through it and it was still in color." I waited for his response. He probably thought I was crazy. If the situation had been reversed, I wouldn't have believed him. But this was real.

Zack threw his head back and laughed. "Dude, nice try, but I'm not stupid."

Terri jumped up. "He's not lying! It's true!"

Zack laughed even more. "Aw man, this is hilarious. Terri, you're so cute. Guys, seriously, I'm not gullible."

I was annoyed. "Fine! See for yourself." I tossed him the ring, which he caught in the air.

He looked through the little hole, jumped, and threw the object back at me. "What the hell *is* that thing?" he asked, staring wide-eyed at it.

"I'm not sure, but all we know is that it spots things that aren't normal, and it's called the what? A-e-greis?" I pointed to the engraved letters.

Zack squinted at the letters. "No. That's aegris. Dude, that thing is messed up. We need to show Emmett and Livia."

After showing Emmett, who went bug-eyed and

dropped the aegris, and Livia, who screamed and backed away, we tried to figure out how this could be possible. Livia started questioning first. "Wait, so this bird? You said it was red?"

"Yeah. Have you seen it before?" I asked, hoping to finally get an explanation. After all, I'd been there such a short time.

"No. This island has only chickadees and seagulls, maybe a sandpiper here or there, but nothing like you're describing," Emmett said. "Here, let me see that."

I passed him the aegris, and he turned it over in his hands. It shone and glistened in the light. He looked through the hole, made a disgusted face, and gave it back. "That thing is plain *messed up*."

I stared at it, wondering how this could be possible. It seemed like a dream, but based on everyone else's dumbfounded looks, I could tell they couldn't believe their eyes either. *How could it be possible? Is it some kind of thing that tells what everything will look like two thousand years from now? Or maybe it's a portal to another dimension. Except it's so small you can only see what it looks like, not go through it. Maybe it was something that wasn't meant for me to find. Maybe something that someone hid to protect it.*

"Jayce, what happened to your hand!" Livia snapped me out of my swirling thoughts. She grabbed my hand and looked at the cut.

"Uh, yeah, it's really fine. I just cut it badly when I was trying to dig this thing out from under a thorn bush." I winced when Livia touched my cut.

"Are you okay? That seems like a bad cut," Emmett

said. Livia let go of my wounded hand and intertwined her fingers with my intact one.

"Yeah. I'm no doctor, but I'm sure it'll heal in a couple of days." I looked at my hand one more time then tried to forget about the pain.

We walked to the restaurant for breakfast and talked about when we thought a new kid would come and what he or she would look like.

"I bet in a couple of weeks a girl will come, and she'll complain about everything, you know, like, 'This weather's too hot! This food's terrible! These people aren't cool!'" Livia said as she mimicked an annoyed voice and waved her hands all around, making us laugh.

"I bet a guy's gonna come in a month and he'll be like, 'Yeah, I'm so cool. Everybody totally likes me even though I'm a jerk.'" Zack mimicked actions and voices as Livia had, and we were laughing our heads off and making silly voices and faces.

When we'd calmed down, Emmett, who had been quiet the whole time, spoke up. "Guys?"

"Yeah?" Zack asked, still chuckling a little from our jokefest.

"I've been wanting to tell you there is going to be someone new. My, um, friend, Luna Wilson. She's gonna be here in a couple of hours."

10

"Wait! What was her name again?" I asked, want-ing to make sure I'd heard him correctly.

"Luna Wilson," Emmett said slowly, looking at me with uneasy eyes. "You know her?"

I was processing the name. Wilson sounded familiar. I didn't think I'd ever met a Luna, so I just said, "No, I don't know her." But deep down, I felt something was strange about that name.

At the restaurant, Terri said, "You guys go ahead. I need to show Jayce something." Zack looked at her with a confused face, but she gave him a smile, which prompted a smile from him, and he went in.

She waited until everyone else was inside before she turned to me, a very serious look on her face. "All right, what's up? I can tell what you're thinking. That name's familiar to you, right? Who is she?"

I was startled. I was usually good at hiding my emotions about things like that, but she knew something was wrong. "Nothing. I just didn't hear Emmett right. I wanted to make sure so I didn't call her by the wrong name or confuse her with someone else." I wanted to convince her nothing was wrong.

"You just lied. Tell me, is that name familiar to you or not?"

Terri was putting the pressure on. *How did she know this?* "Okay, fine. The name sounds familiar to me, but I don't remember ever having met a Luna Wilson. The name just sounds like I've heard it before. How could you tell?" I hated when people were trying to get me to tell them something.

Terri paused. "Well, I actually don't know. I just looked at you and could immediately tell something was wrong." She looked puzzled. "Let's eat breakfast. I need food to think."

We went inside. The restaurant was packed. People were at every table eating pancakes and crunchy bacon. My stomach growled at the sight and smell of the hot, delicious food.

Luckily, our friends had staked claim to one of the few open tables. We sat and ordered a feast of waffles, pancakes, and bacon. Our food came quickly, which was surprising especially considering how busy the restaurant was.

"So I'm guessing today is our first work day," I said, forking waffles into my mouth.

"Yeah. After this, we go to Theo, and he gives us our jobs for the day," Zack said, shoving mouth-watering bacon into his already-stuffed mouth.

"Don't worry. It's usually not too much or it's just easy jobs," Livia said.

"Easy for *you* to say. He loves you," Emmett said.

"That's because I actually get my jobs done quickly unlike you two," Livia replied with a smirk.

"What can I say? The jobs are boring, so we try to make them fun," Zack said between bites.

Livia smiled and looked at me. "Just get the jobs done quickly and efficiently even if they're boring and you'll be fine."

We laughed at jokes and stories we told each other as we ate, and we left. We were about to go to Theo to get our assignments, but Zack stopped us. "So Jayce, what did Terri show you?"

Terri and I exchanged looks. She said, "Actually, I was asking Jayce about something because—" She stopped.

I looked at her. She wanted to know if I was okay with telling him. *Wait a second! How'd I know that?* "Well, we think we're able to look at each other and ... know how the other feels and what they're thinking."

"So you can read each other's minds?" Emmett asked.

"No, it's just more like we can guess what the other is thinking. It's not direct mind reading, but we can still tell what's going on in the other's mind," I said, still processing what I said myself.

"Whoa," a baffled Livia murmured.

"Wow! I didn't know all those rumors about twins being able to do stuff like that were true," Zack said.

Terri and I gave each other confused looks. I said, "Neither did we."

II

I talked to Theo and found out I had to work at the shop for an hour, but I'd get to do it with Livia since I was new. Terri and Zack had to collect sticks and logs from the hiking trail for the campfire. Emmett had to help a little in the restaurant before he went to meet Luna when she came.

Working would have been boring, but since Livia was there, it wasn't that bad. When there wasn't anyone who needed help, we'd joke around, laugh, and even play trash-ketball with a crumpled piece of paper.

Livia showed me how to work the register and told me where everything was, and after that, we took turns helping people. One would be at the register while the other would be walking around, looking at stuff, and helping the customers.

During a quiet spell, I asked, "What do you think is the easiest job?"

"Well, getting firewood is pretty easy, but the shop is also. You just stand around and answer easy questions people can't figure out themselves." Livia let out a laugh, and I smiled.

After a few hours, we were done. We walked over to meet Luna, whom Emmett was showing around the island. I noticed Livia was wearing a necklace with a star. "I like your necklace," I said.

"Thanks," she said. "I love necklaces. Sometimes, I think I have too many."

We smiled as we walked to the pool, where Emmett said he would meet us with Luna. I still wondered about that name, that person. I hoped when I saw her it would trigger something in my mind that would give me an idea of why her name seemed familiar.

I saw Zack, Terri, Emmett, and a girl with dark hair. Emmett was talking to her, and when he saw us, he smiled and waved us over.

We jogged over, and Emmett walked up to us. "Hey guys. I'd just finished showing Luna the island when Zack and Terri showed up, then you guys came. Luna, this is Jayce and Livia."

The girl was small, and seemed shy, but she looked strong and somewhat fearless. She seemed almost intimidating, but she said "Hi" in a shy way.

"Hey Luna, nice to meet you," I said, still racking my brain.

She looked at me for a while, and I stared back. Something was strange. She looked as if she were trying to figure something out. *Does she know me, or do I just look familiar to her as she does to me?*

She just kept looking at me and said, "Nice to meet you too."

Livia whispered in my ear, "Is something wrong?"

I was trying to decide whether to tell her. "No."

She shrugged and asked, "What do you guys want to do?"

"I think I might go to the climbing wall," I said since I hadn't been climbing in a long time.

"Emmett, could we play soccer?" Luna asked.

"Sure. I was thinking the same thing. Zack, Terri? Want to join us? We could also get a few older kids to play," Emmett said, knowing Livia would probably go with me.

"All right, then. See you guys later," Zack said.

As Livia and I walked the trail, she told me about her time on the island before I came.

"There used to be another girl here, Audrey, but she left a few months ago when her dad got a job in Michigan. We never really had anything in common anyway. All she would ever do was stay on her phone or do boring stuff, unlike you."

"Do you know if she'll come back?" I asked.

"Probably not. Even if she did, she'd be here for only a little bit, then she'd leave again."

Suddenly, the aegris in my pocket started getting hot. Something was definitely wrong. "Wait a second," I said. I pulled it out. It became even warmer, almost to the point of being too hot. I decided to look through the hole for any signs of the bird or anything new. I searched through leaves and branches for anything I could spot.

"What's wrong?" Livia asked, getting closer to me as if we could look through it at the same time.

"It started to grow really warm, but I have no idea why." I kept looking at the trees, maybe for another bird.

"Is anything in color? What's going on?" Livia asked in an urgent tone.

"I'm trying to find something, but there's nothing."

"Maybe it just got warm from the sun, or maybe there really is nothing."

"It can't be. I was sure it wasn't warm seconds before it heated up. I know there's something."

I looked all around at the trees. Just before I gave up, I saw something that I was surprised I'd missed earlier when I'd taken the aegris out. "Livia?"

Silence for a few seconds. "Yeah?"

"I found something."

"What is it? Something wrong?"

"It's the path. Something's wrong with the trail we're on."

Livia was confused. "You mean it's like in color?"

"No, it's more than that. It's ... glowing."

12

"Glowing?" Livia asked.

"Yeah." I turned around while looking through the aegris. "But when I turn around, the path isn't glowing. It's just lit up the way we're going."

"Hey, I have an idea. Walk down the path the way we're going and tell me what happens."

I headed down the trail, and when I looked back, the path behind me was no longer glowing. When I walked the way we came, the glowing trail got longer. I gasped. "It's creating a path to something. If I go back, the path gets longer."

Livia smiled. "I knew it. Let's follow it."

I grabbed her arm. "Wait. We don't know if this is safe. Don't you think we should get the others?"

She paused. "Honestly, I don't trust Luna, and I know that if we tell the others, she's going to come along too. Something about her isn't right."

"All right. Let's go. But we should probably tell them after."

We started down the path, with me checking it through

the aegris every now and then to make sure we were on the right trail.

A little bit after we passed the climbing wall, which some kids were climbing, I brought our journey to a halt and looked through the magic ring. The path went off the trail deep into the woods.

I looked at Livia. She shrugged. We looked up and down the trail to make sure no one was watching, and we walked in the new direction, but that time, I had my eye looking through the aegris the whole time as Livia followed me.

Looking through the aegris, I saw the campsite in the distance, but the glowing path didn't lead there. Instead, we ended up deep in the woods in a big, open, and glowing space.

"Is this it?" Livia asked.

"I think. There are no other paths." I turned around in circles, but nothing else was glowing except the area we were standing in.

I put the aegris in my pocket, and we started looking around. Livia covered one side while I did the other.

Eventually, she called me over. "This tree is hollow. I kicked a rock that hit the tree, and it made a hollow sound."

I paused. "Let's search the outside of it before breaking into it. I don't want to mess up anything."

We felt the bark, looked for trapdoors, and even dug around some roots. After digging up one weird-looking root, which turned out to be nothing, I looked up and saw something on a branch. "Wait a second," I said. I grabbed the branch. It had the word *Pull* engraved in it. "It says 'pull'." I looked at her, trying to read her expression.

She seemed puzzled, but she shrugged. "It's now or never."

I glanced at the branch again and pulled down on it. It turned out to be much harder to pull than I thought it would be, so I could tell it hadn't been operated in a while. Once I thought I got it down the farthest it could go, we heard a low, rumbling sound that got louder quickly.

"What's going on?" Livia shouted, but I could barely hear her over the sound of machinery.

"I don't know! All I did was just pull the lever!" I had to talk loudly. I hoped no one else on the island heard the noise.

I scanned the area, and right in the middle of the space we were standing in, a huge mound of rocks was forming. My hands grew numb. It didn't look possible. Eventually, an opening started to form. It grew bigger and bigger until the whole mound of rocks looked like a cave leading somewhere below. We couldn't see through a thick mist in the cave to tell what was inside.

I glanced at Livia. Her eyes were wide open. We stayed close together and walked toward the cave. She studied my eyes and reached her hand into the mist. When her fingers felt the fog, she gasped and pulled her hand back.

"It's so hot! It burned me!" she said, holding her fingers.

I reached forward slowly, prepared to have my fingers boiled, but my hand went through the mist with no pain. I pulled it out.

"I don't see what you mean. Maybe we should get our friends," I said. "I'll stay here and make sure nothing happens." I put my hand through one more time. "You should get the others. I wouldn't want this mist to leak out and hurt you or anything if I went."

"Okay. Stay safe," Livia said as she ran back into the woods.

After a few minutes, I put my hand back into the mist. It felt thick and cool but not wet. I wondered what was on the other side. *Maybe I should look.* It felt like a force was slowly pulling me into the cave. I was in a trance. I was so curious to see what was inside. *I don't think Livia would mind if I checked it out. The mist doesn't hurt me anyway.* Even though that didn't make sense, I kept going through.

When my head went through, I felt I was walking through water, but I wasn't wet, and I could breathe even though the air was thick. After walking sluggishly for what I'd guess was about five feet, I stepped out of the mist and into a cave that was just a little bit taller than I was. A dim light illuminated the room, but I couldn't see where it was coming from. There was a strange feeling in the air that seemed full of energy, as if I might be electro-cuted any second.

As I walked deeper into the cave, still in what seemed a trance, I scanned the area. I saw something shimmer-ing, almost glowing, at the end of the cave on a small rock pillar. As I neared it, the glow took the shape of a round object with a small chain. When I got to the pillar, I saw it was an amulet of some sort of pure gold with an oval, fiery, reddish-orange stone in the middle. I saw intricate flame designs around the fiery stone filling the blank space be-tween it and the edges. The small chain was also gold, and the whole thing looked old, maybe ancient, but not damaged or dirty.

I wondered how long it had been there and how it had ended up in the mysterious cave. I grabbed it, and it seemed all the glowing light was sucked into the fiery stone. It grew warm in my hands.

The cave got a little darker. I put the amulet in my pocket and dashed out of the cave.

But there was something wrong. I wish I had paid attention to the aegris burning hot in my pocket before walking out.

13

I walked back through the mist and searched for the branch that opened the cave. I found it and pushed the lever up. The loud rumbling started again, and the mist started to slowly disappear as the cave crumbled down until it was just a flat piece of land again.

I walked back to the trail and pulled out the aegris, which was cool, and looked at the trail through it. The glowing path was gone. I took out my notepad and drew pictures of and made notes about my discoveries—the cave, the amulet, and the aegris.

I saw my friends approaching. Livia ran up and whispered, "What did you do? I told you to stay there."

I talked in a low voice. "I went inside the cave, but don't worry, it's not dangerous. The glowing path is gone now."

Zack, Terri, Emmett, and Luna walked up. "Livia," Terri said, "are you gonna show us?"

"Actually, I already went in there. There's nothing special." I was lying. "I just came back out and closed it."

Livia shot me an annoyed look. "I guess we should show them the cave."

"I'll show you guys the way," I said. "But first, did you guys hear a loud rumbling sound a few minutes ago?"

"No," Emmett said.

"Weird how no one on the island heard it," Luna said quietly.

We walked to the open area, and I pulled the branch. It responded easily that time. The loud noise of machinery started again, and the others stared in shock as they watched the huge cave rise and form.

The foggy mist seemed thicker than before. Everyone's eyes were huge. For a minute, no one moved. Zack walked to it and was reaching out to touch it. I jumped in front of him and pushed him back. "Stop! It's going to burn you," I cried and reached behind into the mist. "You can try to touch it if you want, but it's probably going to hurt you. It didn't burn me, though."

"Let me try." Zack reached around me and slowly put his hand into the fog. He pulled his hand back quickly, cried out, and cradled his hand. "You're right. It hurts!"

Emmett carefully stuck his into it, yelped, and yanked his hand back. He shook it due to the pain. "Do you know why it doesn't hurt you?"

"Not a clue," I said. "I just reached in there and it didn't hurt me."

Terri walked toward the mist, but before she could reach out, Zack grabbed her. "Don't try it. It burned me!"

"Zack, just let me try this," she said and moved around him. She cautiously extended her fingers into the fog but didn't react. "It doesn't hurt me."

"Really?" I asked.

"Must be because you guys are related," Emmett

said. "Or maybe because you're twins. But why did it let you two?"

No one could answer that.

Terri shoved one arm in and then the other. She did the same with a leg. "Strange."

After letting Terri see the inside of the cave, which she described as empty and dark, I pulled the branch down and the cave disappeared as it had before. We headed back down the trail in a little parade, all silent, deep in thought. About halfway down the trail, Luna asked, "What now?"

Everybody was quiet. No one knew what to do. I decided to speak up. "Livia, do you want to start on that tree house project we were thinking about?" I made it sound as if it had been a normal summer day for typical teens.

"Uh, yeah, sure."

I could tell she was still trying to process everything that had happened.

Farther down the trail, Livia and I separated from our friends when it split in two. We got to the shed that held our gear, and Livia retrieved a bunch of tools and wood.

She gave me a belt to hold most of the tools, and I helped her carry some of the supplies to the tree where the ziplines started. I thought we'd have to haul the wood up piece by piece, but she pointed to a rope dangling from the tree a few feet away.

"Don't you ever worry someone is gonna find this tree and mess with all the stuff in it?" I asked, dragging some wood over to the rope.

"Nope. It may not be super deep in the woods, but no one ever comes to this spot. They always stay on or near the trail." She tied up a stack of wood. "Could you do me a favor? Climb up there and pull up this rope. There's a pulley up there. Once it gets up there, untie it and set the wood on some branches. Send the rope down and I'll tie up more stuff."

"Got it." I started up the tree.

I was almost to the top when some branches started shaking. I saw some kind of dark figure quickly disappear as branches shook farther and farther away until I couldn't hear or see it anymore. Startled, I hastily got to the top. and looked around. A few small branches had been snapped, and a few nails were still rolling around on some wood, but the figure had left no other signs that it had been there.

I found the rope and pulled the wood up with lots of grunting. I set the pile aside and untied the rope. Every few minutes, I'd look around to see if the mysterious figure was watching.

I let the rope down to Livia, but I felt uneasy doing so. I got my pocketknife out and kept it in my hand as I kept pulling the rope around the pulley, trying not to cut myself.

When I felt a tug on the rope, I knew Livia was tying up a new pile. I sat on the platform and leaned against a branch, knife in hand. I kept watch as I waited for Livia to bring up the next load, hoping that whatever was up there had gone for good. I watched with anxious eyes as I saw the rope move around and tug. My eyes kept wandering to the nearest branches and trees, hoping nothing was around.

I was pulling the rope up when I heard a branch snap. I heard a faint whisper but couldn't tell what it said. I dropped the rope, hoped Livia was out of the way of the falling woodpile, and held my knife out. My heart started to beat faster and faster. I waited for another sound.

I saw something to my left. I turned and saw the figure rush around to the right. I tried to follow its direction with my knife just in case it lunged at me. As I saw the figure randomly appear from left to right, almost seeming as if it were teleporting, I tried to make out a shape, face, person—anything. But all I could see was shadow.

I wondered if Livia was going to come up or not. I was scared out of my mind. I probably looked like a madman, eyes wide with fear, jerking around at any movement or sound.

A flash of darkness came from the right. I tried to stab whatever it was, but it smacked me in the head. Pain exploded in my brain. I grabbed a branch to keep my balance. I could feel warm blood trickling through my hair. I was dizzy. I couldn't see the figure, but spots started to appear in my vision. After a few seconds, the pain wasn't that bad; it just somehow made my brain turn to mush. I couldn't process what was happening correctly.

I heard Livia shouting my name as she climbed up. The figure swooped by again, but that time, I was too weak to strike. Pain shot up my arm. I saw that the being had torn a part of it. My knife dropped. I started to stumble as I moaned and grabbed my hurt arm.

My vision was fading. I was about to fall out of the tree just as I saw Livia rushing to climb up and reach to grab me.

14

I slowly came to. My eyes struggled to focus. I was on a cot. When I looked around, I saw a few armchairs and a rug in the room I was in. Tables were here and there; some had tools on them and others had what looked like plans, blueprints. A few lights and lamps illuminated the place. A bulletin board took up almost one entire wall. It contained plans for tree houses, maps, pictures of what seemed like strange patterns in trees, mysterious sightings, and a photo of what seemed to be a shadow caught by a security camera.

I saw the bag Livia had brought out of the shed the night we went ziplining slumped against a wall, and I saw more pictures and journal entries, tools, and a bunch of other items I couldn't quite make out. I saw Livia at one table writing something.

"Livia?" I asked in a faint voice. "Where am I?"

"Underground. It's my hiding and hangout place." She walked over and gave me some water. I sat up. My head was pounding. I could feel a bandage on my head and arm.

"It took me forever to get you back down the tree. I had to get you down using some ropes and pulleys. There were some scary moments when I thought I'd drop you. The blood wouldn't stop coming out of your head. At one point, it started oozing some black liquid, but I have no clue what it was. I have a first aid kit down here, so I cleaned you up and wrapped your injuries. You can take them off if you want. You're not bleeding anymore."

"How ... how much time has passed?" I tried to remember what had happened.

"Just a few hours or so. After patching you up, I let you rest here. I told the others we were gonna camp out in the woods for a night or so. They're cool with it."

We were quiet. I removed the bandage on my head.

"Does anyone else know about this place? How did you get it?"

"No one knows about this place."

"How did you make it? And... what is in those pictures?" I pointed to the shadow lurking in the corner of the photo.

She was silent for a bit. "I'll be honest. I've always known this island wasn't normal. I've never told the others because I didn't want to cause a commotion, but I've never found anything as crazy as you did. Just small, strange stuff, like that mysterious shadow. I knew about it mainly because the strange things happen only in the woods. I didn't make this room. I found this bunker a long time ago. I noticed all the trees leaned the same direction toward a certain tree. I saw that the huge roots were loose, so I ripped them away, and a tunnel led to here. The bunker was empty besides the tables and chairs, so I snuck some stuff in here and made it mine."

I couldn't believe she'd known about the strangeness

all along. "How did you sneak all this in without getting caught?"

"For an uptight, on-the-ball boss, Theo sure is oblivious to people sneaking in after hours. It's weird. I creep in during the night all the time and he never seems to notice, but when I sneak in after 5:30 in the morning, he catches me every time. It's super weird, but it's none of my business. Since he thinks we're on the trail, I was able to lower you from the tree with a rope and sneak us both in."

I started to get up. I was a little dizzy still. "We need to tell the others."

"Don't go."

"Why not?"

"You can't leave. There's a ghostly being stalking you. If it finds you again, I'm not sure I'll be able to save you. You have to hide out here until it stops searching for you. Also, they'll see your injuries. They'll wonder what happened, and we'll have to tell them about all this."

"Can you at least tell them to be careful because we saw something that tried to hurt me?"

"I'll go tell them and get some food. That sound good?"

"Well, I trust you, but are you sure that whatever that thing is won't come back?"

"I'm positive! Nobody knows about this place except you and me."

She dashed through the room and up the tunnel to the surface.

As I waited impatiently, I checked out Livia's plans. There were some on tree houses, redoing the bunker, making new ziplines, and more. I paced as I waited for Livia. I was hoping that whatever it was wouldn't find me.

After what I'd guess to be twenty or thirty minutes, Livia came back with sandwiches.

She gave me one and said, "Bad news."

Uh oh. "What is it?"

"You're not the only one who was attacked. While they were walking on the trail, the being attacked them. Terri has a gash on her face but nothing else. She passed out too. Zack said they told Theo she slipped and cut her face on a rock. She's okay, though. Don't worry."

My eyes were wide open in shock. "I hope she's okay. Why is this happening to us?" I asked even though I knew Livia didn't know. "Do you think this is connected to the fact only Terri and I were able to touch the mist?"

"Probably."

We were silent as we held hands.

She suddenly turned to me, eyes wide. "Jayce, I just realized something."

"What?"

"There's one person who didn't feel the mist to see if it hurt. Luna."

I realized what I hadn't noticed before.

15

We ate the sandwiches, and I slept on the cot while Livia slept on a couch. I couldn't sleep well; I was trying to figure out everything that had happened that day. I rolled over and felt the amulet in my pocket. *It would be a nice necklace for Livia.*

I decided to close my eyes and reach out to Terri, to read her feelings. I felt fear and pain. She was scared of what would happen the next day. I tried to talk to her, but she didn't answer. She shivered and hummed a mysterious tune. That sent chills down my back, but I figured it was something she'd heard on the radio. I wanted to help her. I decided that the next day I'd go to her whether a being was stalking me or not. Before I could think of anything else, I fell asleep.

When I woke up, I realized I'd slept in some and Livia had been at the table again.

"What are you doing?"

"Planning a few things for the tree house and figuring out what's going on by trying to connect the things I've seen before to the things you're seeing now. It's a good thing you slept in. After that hit to the head you took, you needed rest."

I waited until I was less sleepy before getting out of bed and putting my shoes on. "I'm going to go see Terri."

Livia spun around. "Don't! You're in danger. Terri is safe with the others. They can protect her. If not, I can bring her here."

I was determined to see her. "I don't care if there's danger. I'm going to see her. She's my sister. I need to take care of her."

I headed out the tunnel. Livia followed me reluctantly. At the end of the tunnel, I pushed up on some thick roots. After letting my eyes get used to the sunlight, I crawled out of the ground like a zombie.

Livia emerged and put the roots back in place.

"How do we get back to the field?" I asked.

"It's a little ways over there. I'll show you."

After going through trails, trees, and bushes, we finally made it to the clearing. I scanned the area and saw people walking on the paths and some adults playing volleyball but no Terri.

We checked the shop, but my grandfather said she had left with Zack, Emmett, and Luna a while before.

We went to the beach and saw adults and kids at play. I spotted Terri way down at the end of the beach staring at the ocean.

We walked up. "Terri?"

My sister spun around and looked me up and down. A bandage on her cheek ran to her neck and nose. She jumped up and ran to me. She hugged me and didn't let go.

"Jayce, I was attacked."

"I know. Me too. It's gonna be okay."

"I'm scared," she whispered. I could sense she was about to cry. She was worried about me deeply.

"Don't be," I replied to her thought, trying to calm her down. "I'm here now. We're gonna be fine. Our friends will help us."

Livia put her hand on Terri's shoulder. "Hey, it's gonna be okay. I'll help protect you and Jayce."

Terri let go of me. She sniffled and nodded.

I mouthed, *"Where are the others?"* to Livia. She just glanced at me and shrugged.

"Do you know where Emmett and Zack are?" Livia asked Terri in a sweet voice, sounding like a mother trying to cheer up her daughter.

"I think they went to look for Luna. When we were helping at the pool, she disappeared. I wanted to stay here where lots of people are so I didn't get attacked again."

I almost shivered when she said Luna's name. She was so mysterious. The fact she'd disappeared without a trace was even stranger.

Then it hit me. "Wilson!" Like a wild lion set loose from its cage, the memory leaped out of my head and through my mouth. "Terri, do you remember Mom having that long phone call a few weeks before we came here?"

"I think so. Why?"

"I remember her mentioning Luna's last name, Wilson. That's why it sounded familiar. When Emmett mentioned her name, it dinged in the back of my mind, but I couldn't pull it out."

I tried to remember what my mother had said during

that conversation, which I had secretly listened to. "Ugh. I'm trying to remember it."

As I was racking my brain, the memory of the call flooded over me. I remembered my mom trying to speak in a low voice. I remembered her mentioning my dad's name, John, and I remembered snatches of the conversation. "The least you could do is protect them ... I'm just not sure if they'll be safe here. They're getting older, and I need help. Ever since John left, it's been so hard ... Please get the Wilsons too. We need as much help as we can. I know he'll come for them."

That's where the name had come from. I struggled to remember more.

"We can't let them know what's happening, not until a few weeks have passed, not now ... If he comes after them, you might need to give them something for defense even if it means telling them the truth. Even if it means that John has to come back ... Please get the Wilsons, but whatever you do, don't let their daughter handle this ... Okay, please protect them. I can't thank you more."

I told them everything I'd remembered. "I don't know why I couldn't remember what she said until now, but I'm positive that's what she said."

"Who's 'he'?" Livia asked.

"She never said, but from what it sounded like, I think she was referring to the figure that attacked us. As for the person she was calling, I have no idea. It might've been Theo, but I'm not sure." I replayed my memory of that phone conversation many times. I didn't want to forget it again, and I was searching for any clues about what was happening to us.

Terri spoke up. "Didn't you say Mom said, 'Don't let their *daughter* handle this'?"

"That's Luna, isn't it?" I asked no one in particular.

"Probably. She might not be who we think she is," Livia said.

We were all trying to sort it out in our minds, but so much was missing; it was a jigsaw puzzle with half the pieces missing.

"I'll speak to Theo tonight, and I'm gonna try to figure some things out," I declared.

"Jayce, I don't think you should. Maybe this is something we shouldn't get involved in," Terri said in a worried tone of voice.

"We need to find some kind of answer even if it's barely anything. Something big is going on, something dangerous. We need as much info and help as we can," I said. "We also need to warn Emmett and Zack of all this, especially about Luna."

"Good plan," Livia said. "Let's find them."

16

We walked to the fields, where my grandfather met us.

"Where have you guys been? I need someone to help me restock the shop," he said, looking slightly agitated.

"I'll do it," Terri said, glancing at me. "You guys go ahead."

I mouthed *"Thank you,"* and Livia and I walked to the pool, which turned out to be empty. We saw Zack came out of a shed carrying pool supplies.

"Where is everyone?" I asked, looking around the deserted area.

"There were others here until some people came and announced a contest was going on. Everyone left, and that's when we lost Luna. Emmett went to look for her while I stayed here to clean up a bit and wait for you guys," he said.

"We need to find Emmett," Livia said. "We have something to tell you two, and it's actually good Luna isn't here because we can't tell her."

Zack looked serious. "What's wrong?"

"Just bring us to Emmett," I said.

We located Emmett and took him to a hidden part of the field where no one would find us. We told them what had happened. I replayed the memory in my mind and said the exact words my mom had spoken. "I have no idea how it came to my mind, but it just hit me, and I remembered."

"We also think that his mom was referring to Luna," Livia said. "We need to be careful around her."

Emmett just stared at the ground. "Luna isn't bad ..."

Zack put a hand on his shoulder. "She might not be who you think she is."

Emmett's face changed. "No! She's not bad! They can't be talking about her. Not Luna!"

Livia started to talk. "Emmett—"

"No! I know she's not evil! Either you're lying or you heard your mom wrong! Why would she know about Luna's family anyway?" He threw the question at me, daring me to answer.

"Listen, Emmett," I said, "she might *not* be bad, but right now, some strange things are going on, and we aren't sure whom we can trust. My family might know her, but for now, all we know is that we're in danger and need help."

"Fine," Emmett said. "But we still need to find her."

"Guys, we also need to stick together," Zack said. "With this crazy stuff happening, none of us should be alone. I'll get Terri once she's done with her job."

"All right then, let's go," Livia said. She walked toward the open area, but before she could, I stopped her.

"Hey Livia, I found this earlier and I wanted to give it

to you." I took out the amulet. "Since you like necklaces so much."

She smiled as she took the amulet. "Thanks! I love it. It looks really cool."

She kissed me on the cheek and put the necklace on.

A few moments passed. Livia's face scrunched up. She gasped. "Ah, it's getting really hot!" she said as she jumped back.

I felt myself being blown back. I saw her go up in flames. I covered my eyes.

17

I moved my hands, trying to see past all the heat.
Livia was on fire. I stared into the inferno and screamed
her name. Once. Twice. Many times. A million thoughts
went through my head. *It's all my fault. I should've known
the amulet wasn't normal. She's dead because of me.* My
whole body was numb. A little voice in the back of my head
was saying, *You killed her. You're a murderer.*

I looked at my friends. They were safe, but their eyes
were wide with fear. Guilt and sadness filled me. I could
feel tears forming in my eyes despite the heat. I felt like a
murderer. I should have known it would have had some
kind of power. I wanted to help, but there was nothing I
could do. I watched as tears cascaded down my face. I
knelt down and covered my eyes.

I heard someone calling my name. I opened my eyes
and looked up. The flames were starting to diminish, and
I could see a figure underneath. *Could it be possible?* I
watched in amazement as the flames diminished until
there was nothing but a person standing there. The ground
all around her was intact somehow, no signs of damage.

"Livia?" I asked weakly.

She looked at me. Her hair was redder, even fiery. Her eyes had turned a bright red as well. She looked full of energy, not hurt at all. She also seemed to be stronger, almost like a whole new person. Maybe not even human.

"Uh, what … just happened?" Zack asked.

I peered at her. "Is … is that you, Livia?"

She looked at her hands and then her whole body. "I … I think so. But I feel … weird."

"How could she be okay?" Emmett asked. "She was just on *fire!*"

"It didn't hurt," Livia said. "I saw the fire, I heard shouting, but here I am!"

We stared at her for a few minutes.

"Where did you find this … this thing?" she asked.

"I found it in the cave while you went to find the others. I didn't want to tell you since we were around Luna, and I just didn't trust her. I haven't since I met her. It seemed to have some kind of energy, but I thought it wouldn't harm anyone. I was in a trance. I didn't know it would be bad." I was afraid she'd hate me.

But Livia didn't say a word; she just looked at me wide-eyed. I couldn't read her expression well, but it seemed she had figured something out. She raised her hand, and for a second I thought she had something in it, but it was just her hand. I wondered what she was doing until she closed her eyes, scrunched up her face, and looked as though she was concentrating hard. Then her hand caught on fire.

She opened her eyes and gasped. She raised her other hand, which also lit up with flames. She let the flames jump from one hand to other. She closed her eyes, and the blaze gradually burned out. When she opened her eyes, they were their usual blue color.

No one said anything. Livia grabbed the amulet and took a long look at it. I walked up and slowly put my hand on her shoulder, being careful so I wouldn't catch on fire.

"This is—" Zack tried to formulate his thoughts. "This is crazy! I can't believe this." He ran his hands through his hair.

"We need to tell Terri about this," I said, taking my hand off Livia and looking at her. "Let's hope you can control that fire. We don't want to draw any attention or burn anything down."

She made the fire flicker around her hands again and said, "I think I can."

Livia made a fireball and let it roll up and down her arm. She made two more and juggled all three.

"Dude, now you're just showing off," I said in a teasing tone.

"Just having a little fun here. I need to get used to it anyway. I don't know what would happen if I took off the amulet, so let's not take any chances," Livia said.

"Probably for the best," I said.

"Where did all of this come from?" a bewildered Zack asked.

"I'm going to talk to my grandfather tonight. He has to know *something*," I said. "It will be surprising if he doesn't know anything strange about this island. He's owned it for years."

"But first," Emmett said, "we need to find Terri and tell her about this, and don't forget we need to find Luna."

Before anyone could do anything else, a bunch of birds

flew from the trees. It became strangely windy, and there was a mysterious feeling among us, a presence in the air. It started to get foggy. We looked at each other. Without thinking, I ran to the big opening on the island, and everyone followed. No one was there except Terri.

"Jayce? Zack?" she called out.

"We're over here!" Zack yelled.

The fog had become extremely dense. My heart was beating wildly. Something strange was going on. *Where is everyone?* I could barely see anything through the fog except my friends and Terri, who caught up to us.

"What's happening?" I shouted. The wind was howling.

"Don't know! I walked out of the shop and nobody was out here. Then this fog came out of nowhere!" Terri's eyes were wide with fear.

I couldn't see anything outside the big circle of fog that surrounded us. We could see the ground and each other, but that was it. We huddled close.

Livia shouted to me, "*What* is going *on?*"

"I don't know, but something doesn't feel right," I said.

On the other side of the circle, away from us, a figure appeared in the fog. "Guys, look!" I said, pointing.

We all stared at a man coming out of the fog into our opening. We could barely see who he was or what he looked like, but he was clothed in black. We froze. We never took our eyes off the man, who stood and stared at us.

Emmett stepped forward. "Who *are* you?"

The man didn't open his mouth, but his expression changed from blank to stern. It was maddening to wait and see what he was going to do.

He lunged forward though he was far away. While in

midair, he turned into a big cloud, a shadow, no shape. Just floating darkness. It started to zoom toward us, and we all backed away, spreading out a little.

The shadow spoke in a loud, booming, scratchy, even alien voice. "Twins of John, go back to where you came from!" he screamed. The shadow flew toward me. "And I cannot let *you* change this!"

My eyes went wide with fear as the shadow sped closer. It hit me with such force that I couldn't think of anything.

18

I screamed. I felt I was suffocating. I choked and gagged. I couldn't hear a thing. I couldn't see anything but swirling, dark fog.

Soon, I could see an opening in the dark. I moved toward it. I could see the inside of my house on the other side. Somehow, I could walk in the darkness. I did until I got through the hole.

I was in my house. Terri was watching TV, and my mom was seated and reading. They acted as if they hadn't seen me enter through the portal, so I sat by Terri, confused as could be.

The phone rang. She answered it. Her eyes opened wide. "Your father's coming back home! My sweet John is coming back!" She was jumping for joy as she spoke.

Terri was so happy, but I wasn't sure how to feel about it. *Is this real? What happened?*

A man came through the door. My mother ran up and hugged him. Terri smiled as he embraced her. He looked at me. "Jayce? I'm home."

I stared at him. It didn't seem right. I'd seen him only when I was a baby, so I didn't know what he looked like before, but it didn't seem he was my dad. I remembered that my mom had told us he'd gone into the army when we were small. But why had he come back? *No. This isn't real. It can't be. This isn't my dad. This is not my dad. I need to find a way out.*

The dream melted away. I was in darkness again. I was sweating. I had no clue what was going on.

"Hello?" I yelled. No response. I heard panting and heavy footsteps and turned in that direction. I saw my sister running toward me. "Terri?"

She ran up. "Jayce!" She hugged me. "Jayce! They're all dead!"

"What?" I cried out in shock and amazement.

"Our friends! He killed them all! We need to get out of here, leave this island. It'll be safer. We'll be okay. It'll all be over."

Wait a second. That doesn't sound like something Terri would say. If our friends had died, nothing would ever be okay for Terri. This isn't real. Don't let it fool you.

"No. This isn't real. You aren't my sister."

Terri pulled back. She looked disappointed, which almost made me feel guilty, but then I remembered not to believe any of it was real.

An evil and mysterious voice whispered in my ears, "I cannot let you help them. Watch your sister suffer!"

Terri threw back her head and screamed. She fell.

"Terri!" I ran to her but was flung back and landed on nothing but darkness. My heart didn't care if this was just a hallucination. I had to save Terri.

"Please! I'm not helping anyone." I rose. "I don't know what you're talking about! Just don't torture my sister."

"Enough!" the voice demanded. Terri screamed again. She was clutching her stomach. I wanted to help her, but the darkness wouldn't let me move. It was horrible to watch and listen helplessly. I covered my face and ears and fell to my knees. The sounds were unbearable. Terri screamed again, and I let out a frustrated scream of my own. I couldn't hear anything else. I kept my hands over my face.

"I will leave you be for now," said the voice. "But I am taking what you need most."

I could sense something happening, like a being passing through me. I parted my hands, and I could see the darkness lifting. I was back in the opening with all my friends standing around me. Tears were streaming down my face.

"Jayce!" Terri shouted and ran to me to help me up. Her eyes were puffy from crying.

"Is ... is that you? The real you?" I asked weakly.

"What are you talking about? It's me, your sister," she said, helping me up. I was beyond dizzy.

Livia came up to me, her face red and wet from tears. "Darkness consumed you, and we didn't know what to do. I couldn't do anything with fire because you were inside it. Then the shadow dropped you, and you look like it did something terrible to you." She held me close.

"It was terrible ... I think it was messing with my mind, causing hallucinations. My dad came home, but it didn't seem like the man who was once my father. And Terri was being tortured." I sniffled. I must have looked like a complete idiot wiping my eyes while my friends were watching. "It was the worst experience of my life." My head ached from Terri's horrible screams hammering my head.

"Did anything else happen?" Zack asked.

I suddenly remembered the voice's last words. "He ... he told me he was going to take something—I don't know what."

I saw Livia reach for the amulet around her neck. It was still there.

"Why does he want you and Terri?" Emmett asked. "He seemed to mostly hate you. Did you do something we don't know about?"

"No. I don't know why he hates us," I said. "But one thing's for sure, he knows my dad. The man said my father's name."

"What now?" Zack asked.

"Now we have something to fight him back with," Livia said. She set her hand on fire.

Terri backed away and let out a squeal. She was clearly terrified. We'd forgotten to tell her about the fire thing. Livia realized that, and she made the flames die. "Don't worry! It doesn't hurt me. We forgot to tell you, but Jayce found an amulet, and apparently, it gives me these divine fire powers." She shot a fireball into the air, caught it on its return, and snuffed it out. Terri stayed in her spot, away from the fire.

Zack looked up at the sky. "Guys, it'll be dark soon. We should find Luna."

Zack was right. The sun was setting. I saw people walking out of buildings and from the beach and trail, acting as if it were a normal day, nothing strange going on.

"The contest was held at the beach," Emmett said. "Let's look there first."

We headed out. I put my hands in my pockets. I felt my notepad and pen. I vowed to write down everything that night. Then my eyes went wide. I realized I no longer had the aegris.

19

Over the next few days, I tried to work up the nerve to question my grandfather about the island. *Will he laugh? Tell me it was the truth? Get so mad at what trouble I've caused and kick me off the island?*

I guessed he knew something was going on anyway. Whenever he spoke to me those days, I guess I was more quiet than usual or had a weird look on my face trying to figure out how to ask him. He'd have a puzzled expression on his face.

I'll have to tell him sooner or later.

I spent those days recovering and trying to figure out what had happened. Nothing strange occurred, so my friends and I just used it as downtime, but every little strange thing startled us.

I tried to remember everything that had happened over the course of the week. The shadow, the aegris, Terri's and my ability to sense each other's thoughts, my grandfather having a cane even though he could walk just fine, the red bird, the cave, the amulet, Livia's bunker, Terri and I being attacked, and my being engulfed in darkness. *And almost dying.* I was more scared than I'd ever been.

With all those things having happened one right after another, it was tough to sit down and think about them calmly, rationally.

But I was as happy as I could be to have a few normal days. I got my jobs done and hung out with my friends as a normal teenager would. The only difference was that we were all jumpy, suspicious, and alert for anything to happen.

We'd found Luna by the end of that crazy day, but it seemed as if she had come out of nowhere. She claimed she'd followed everyone to the contest and thought Emmett would know she was going, but I could tell she was lying. I could see it in her eyes. *What's going on in her head? What's she thinking?*

Terri stayed close to me those next few days. I didn't know if it was to protect me or be protected by me. She'd sensed I was nervous about talking to our grandfather about it and was just making excuses for not doing it. She was right.

I hated and loved our sensory powers.

I had told the others the aegris was gone. We concluded it must have been the object the shadow said he'd take. I told Livia to make sure that nothing happened to the amulet and that no one noticed it. Though she found out she could take it off with no harm, she kept it around her neck but tucked into whatever top she was wearing.

Some days after our jobs were done, Livia and I would go into the woods so she could practice her fire powers, and one of the others joined us on occasion. We decided on having her practice in the open area where the cave was since it was so deep in the forest. I opened the cave a few times just to check if anything had changed. Nothing ever did.

After doing countless tests and exercises, we found out more about the fiery amulet's powers. She could snuff out flames anywhere at will, which could prevent uncontrollable fires. We had also learned the hard way that no one else could wear the amulet. I tried putting it on, but instead of anything fire-like happening, it just got very hot and burned my neck.

She practiced shooting fireballs and fire arrows at rocks I'd toss into the air. She could shoot anything made of fire. The bigger it was, the harder and longer it took for her to conjure it up and shoot it, but she learned to fling flaming balls, arrows, even a bit of lava if she focused super hard, though it drained her energy when she did. At times, she'd just erupt flames out of her hands as if she were a human flamethrower, and she'd jokingly chase me around without burning me. Her fires never developed any smoke, which was helpful.

We bonded more during those times. We talked more about our lives on the mainland. We usually talked more about my life since talking about hers depressed her. But some days, she'd talk about happy things and good times. Her family owned a big woodcutting and shipping company, which is why she could get the supplies and wood for her tree houses. She'd learned from her cousins how to build such amazing things with ease.

I told her about my school and friends, but they weren't nearly as fun as my new ones. None of them ever liked what I liked to do. They just played sports and games all day—nothing else. I gamed and played sports too, but I did much more. I liked heading out and having fun, climbing, and being free rather than staying inside and keeping the world outside. Livia loved hearing my stories as much as I loved telling them.

One day during our afternoon training, Livia was shooting fireballs way up in the air, waiting for a little bit, and then catching them gingerly. She said, "You'll have to talk to him tonight. It's now or never." She raised her arm and shot three medium fireballs straight into the air one after the other.

I was confused. "Did Terri tell you?"

"Yeah, but it's still pretty obvious. You haven't told us anything about your grandfather yet." She looked up. "It'll be dark in a few hours. When he's done with his work, *talk to him.*" She looked up just as the fireballs were coming down. Instead of catching them, she raised her arm and they all disappeared into her hand.

"Okay, fine. I'll talk to him, but what should I say? I'd have to explain so much."

"Just tell him what's happened since you got here. He might be able to explain some things." She picked up some of her stuff. "Let's go find the others."

We went to a campfire that night, the third one for Terri and me in the week we'd been there. I had my eyes glued to the area surrounding the beach, checking for anything strange. After a long time of nothing catching my eye, I decided to just enjoy the night. I'd had about three normal days at that point, so I didn't care about the dark ocean or the forest. I just had a fun time with my friends. At some moments, I thought maybe everything had gotten back to normal, but then I remembered all that had happened. There was no way all of it was gone.

At least once every day, I'd see a flash of red—the bird. One day, during Livia's fire training, it even landed on my shoulder, so I got to show it to Livia. It stayed around and watched Livia's fire tricks.

And Livia and I became closer than ever, and I became closer with the others too.

At the campfire, we all laughed and talked about funny stories and sang songs with our guitarist. I tried to duplicate Zack's special kind of s'more, or as he called it, "The ultimate s'more of all time."

I got all sandy from wrestling with the guys. I lost every time, but they taught me a few moves. Zack had been a champion in his division the previous year, which explained why he could pin me so quickly.

That got us talking about our favorite sports. For Zack, it was wrestling of course. Emmett liked football. Terri couldn't go a week without volleyball. Luna liked soccer, and as I'd learned during one of her training sessions, Livia's sports were lacrosse and tennis. I loved playing third base on my baseball team. We all loved sharing and hearing about competitions and games we'd won, and I learned a little about lacrosse.

After more chatter and meeting some new people, Terri and I were too tired to carry on. We said goodnight and walked back to our room.

The shop closed right before dinner, but my grandfather had given us keys to just about everything on the island though we weren't sure why he trusted us so much.

I felt bad about keeping secrets from him. I decided to spill the beans that night.

We entered the shop and locked up behind us. We wound our way around the delicate items and tried not to make much noise. My sister and I crept up the wooden stairs and went into our room.

Turns out our room wasn't so bad after all. We had decorated our halves of the room the way we liked. Though it was small, it was big enough for two and actually roomier than my bedroom back home. Terri never needed a desk for anything, and as it was on my side of the room, I used it.

A few nights earlier, I was lying in my bed and looking through the skylight about ten feet above me. It was probably only a few feet wide. I thought about asking my grandfather if I could get Livia to make it bigger so I could see the stars before I slept.

What was even better was the ladder I found tucked in my closet. It led up to the roof. There was a small part up there that was about seven feet wide. From the ground, you couldn't see anyone up there, but from that angle, you could see most of the island. I found a foldable chair in the storage room in the hallway and set it up there. I decided it was my place of peace except when Terri would come up and start jabbering away.

I went up there that night, quietly so no one could hear me, and took out my notepad. I made little notes on Livia's training and sketched what I had found. I drew my grandfather's cane that never left his side and put a question mark by it. I wrote about the amulet's abilities and more about the red bird.

I felt my mind being sucked into the notebook. My hand whizzed across the pages. I sketched people I had met, things I had discovered, and plants and animals I'd never seen before. I made notes on all of them. It was my way of finding inner peace and concentration. I felt great when I got to do that.

I even drew things at home I missed and things on the island I'd grown to love, and I even tried to draw my dad. I used the pieces of information about him from my mom and tried to put in down on paper, but it was hard. Even though I'd seen a few pictures of him, producing an image in my head to get on paper was difficult. One of the only main things I know about him were his deep-gray eyes, which neither Terri nor I had; we'd gotten our mother's eyes. I ended up with a halfway finished drawing of a person and a thousand notes on him. I promised myself I'd try hard to find out more until this picture was completed. Until I saw my dad again whether on paper or in real life.

I was sad that I never really had a dad to look after me when I was growing up. I remember my mom telling me that he was the kindest man she'd ever met and that she'd never seen anyone so determined to make his family happy. My mother said he'd had no choice but to leave but never told me why. Even if he had gone into the army, surely he would have come back at some point. He could be dead for all I know.

I wonder if he missed us just as much as we missed him. I didn't care if I'd never met him; I wanted the man who was supposed to be my father with me right where I was sitting. I closed my eyes and tried to think about nothing in an attempt to prevent tears. I breathed deeply, calmed down, and continued drawing.

I drew and wrote, my eyes glued to the pages, for what seemed another half an hour. I was so engrossed in my writing and drawing that I didn't realize someone was standing next to me until he spoke.

"Beautiful night, isn't it?" Theo asked.

I jumped. "Oh yes. I come up here to draw and write. It calms me."

I offered him my chair, but he refused. I noticed he wasn't putting a single ounce of his weight on his cane. Maybe it was just a walking stick.

"I came to say goodnight. Terri said you were up here. She said you wanted to talk to me." He paused. "I see you found the ladder."

I nodded. "Well, I did want to ask you something."

Theo looked at me and raised his eyebrows. "Go on."

"Is there something weird about this island?"

Silence.

"My new friends and I started noticing strange things. Is that normal, or is this island hiding something?"

His face turned grave. He stared at me. "Listen, boy, I need you to tell me everything that happened this past week. I don't care if you told someone you wouldn't tell anyone about it, you have to trust me. I need to hear everything for your safety."

And so it all poured out of my mouth. I told him about the amulet, the aegris, the bird, the shadow, Livia's training—I told him absolutely everything that had happened. When I finished, I looked straight into his eyes, trying to catch some hint of emotion. Nothing.

"Do Emmett, Zack, and Livia know about all this?"

I nodded. "Luna knows only some of it."

His stormy, gray eyes peered into mine. Our stare didn't break until he closed his eyes for a second. He sighed.

"I knew this talk was coming."

I heard him murmur under his breath, "So he *did* get the messages."

My eyes lit up. "Who is *he*?"

"None of your concern at the moment. For now, I need to have a talk with you and your sister, but before I tell her, I need to share a few words with you. Follow me, but I want you to be dead silent." He rose without the help of his cane, grabbed it, and went down the ladder. I followed, nervous as could be.

He led me out of my room and down the hallway to his, where he stopped. "Wait here."

I remembered I'd been forbidden to go in there. The door was slightly cracked open, but I couldn't see anything inside, and I was too afraid to disobey and look. I heard noises and a lock opening. A squeak of some kind of old lid lifting up. Soon enough he was back at the door.

"Since you're old enough now to learn about all this and because you already have one of the others, I want you to have this," he said. He opened his hand. I didn't notice what he was holding until he neared me.

I couldn't believe my eyes.

Another amulet.

20

I took a step back. "Wh ... What? How did you get that?" I was astonished.

"I've had it for years, but I cannot use it anymore. I am too old to fight with it, and it won't even let me put it on now."

I cautiously took the amulet from him.

"The fire amulet also belonged to me, but the aegris was your father's. After I gave him the fire amulet, he had to leave your family, so he hid both. I guess you've found them. But I have no idea where that bird came from. I assume you have figured out how it works, but the aegris helps spot things that can be of assistance, such as the amulets and that bird. It also holds many other uses and secrets within it yet to be discovered."

While he talked, I studied the new amulet. It was similar to Livia's but with a few differences. It was still gold with a chain, but the stone in the middle was, well, it's hard to explain what its color was. It looked a little like space, black with dark blues and purples and maybe a dash of green. The designs around it didn't have any shape as did the flames on Livia's amulet; it had seemingly random, mini swirls and what looked like ancient symbols.

"Who is the shadow guy?" I asked.

"We are not sure. But he has been attacking us ever since we first saw him. He is going after something very valuable, but that is not my job to explain."

"*We*?" I asked, stressing the word.

"Our whole family. Me. You. Your father. Aunts, uncles, older cousins, even your mother, and other families."

"Wait. You mean my father's alive? You're collaborating with him? Is he in the army?"

"I'm afraid not. It was the only thing we could tell you to cover up the truth. Listen closely. Our family is much smarter than the rest of the world as well as a few others. We were smart enough to create these magical items, but we decided to keep them a secret to prevent chaos and confusion if the whole world knew about it.

"We are in an alliance with highly trusted people to secretly save the world from things like the being that attacked you. Our whole family, and the Wilsons, and two other families in New York are at work on a project we call the CPA, the Covert Protection Agency. We secretly protect the world, and no one else knows about it except for those actually in it. It is the families' job to protect everyone else but secretly. So yes, I have been working with your father. But I have not seen him in years."

"What do you mean? Where is he?"

"Very far away, but very close. We work in places around the world, and Luna's family, the Wilsons, have come to help me. Most of the activity has happened in

America, where our main bases are, so we usually stay in this country."

"Please explain more. I just don't understand it. Why does that shadow guy want me?"

"Because he knows you and your friends have the power to stop him. You are the next generation to help us, and you're also the strongest. We are at the peak of our powers, which is you."

"I don't have the power to do anything."

"You have power beyond anything you can imagine, trust me. It is in your blood. There are more amulets, and the shadow is after them all."

"For power?"

"No. So *you* don't take them to have power. Listen carefully. On August 27, toward the end of the summer, there will be an eclipse, what we call the amulet eclipse. When it happens, all the amulets will be destroyed, but we have no idea how that will work. Our few philosophers claimed it was the only thing the shadow could do to destroy them, and we know that only you and your friends have the power to stop him. We found out about it years ago, and your mom sent you here because we needed you. Now. Do not worry. I know your school starts by then, but we have contacted them and said you would not be there for a while.

"When the amulet eclipse occurs, you will have no power to stop the shadow from getting the most important item in the universe, so we need you to get all the amulets. Once you have them all, he will go directly to the place where this item is protected. Go there and take his spirit away."

My mind was in overdrive. So much information. So much to process.

"I know it's a lot to learn in a short time," he said, "but we need you. The only way you can help us is if you know all about it. Some of it is not my job to explain to you, but I promise you will learn much more once you set off on your mission."

"Okay, but what about the Wilsons?"

"Trust them. Even Luna. But be careful around her. She knows about all this, but she can get carried away sometimes."

"What do you mean by—"

"No questions. You will learn later. We are running out of time. I promise you will have help on the way. We have had a few of our people track down where the amulets are, and we will tell you where to go next."

"Do I take my friends?"

"Yes. They are crucial to this mission also. You will need their help."

"I have another question. What's your cane for?"

"Ahh. I see you have noticed I never use it." He held it up. "It is really nothing much compared to the amulets. It is just for self-defense." He twisted it, and it changed into a sword. But it wasn't any normal sword. It looked so sharp. It didn't seem real. I reached out to touch it, but he grabbed my hand. "Do not touch. It does not look like it, but it is actually so hot and sharp that it could cut through or burn anything. I had it enchanted by Luna's father, a good friend."

"Where did all this come from?" I asked.

"It is not important for the moment. You may have

the amulet, but I am keeping my sword, the only weapon I have now that could actually do some *real* damage to someone." His deadly blade transformed back into a cane. "I would let you keep the aegris too, but from what you told me, I assume the shadow figure took it so you could not find any more special items."

I nodded. Then I remembered the gold weapon in my hand, which had grown a little warm. "Now about the amulets," I said. "I tried on Livia's, but it wouldn't work on me. I was forced to take it off. Why?"

"Once an amulet has chosen a person, that person's entire being, the tangible and the intangible, is bound to it. The only thing that can break the spiritual bond is the eclipse." He put his hand over the amulet I was holding. "I have been with this amulet for too long, so I can no longer put it to use, but I can pass it on to you. Do not give this to anyone. It is *your* amulet. That is my only wish for you, okay?"

"Okay." I smiled, a surprising response considering the circumstance. "Would you please tell me what it does before I put it on? When Livia put on her amulet, she exploded into flames."

He smiled. "Put it on and find out. I promise this one will not engulf you in flames."

I was reassured by his words. I closed my eyes and slid the chain around my head, excited for what would happen.

21

The second I felt the amulet hanging from my neck, I slipped into a dark place despite the fact that my eyes were closed. *No! Not the darkness again!*

But it was different. My senses sharpened incredibly. I could feel the presence of everything around me. I felt the walls a few feet away, my grandfather watching me, the floor, ceiling, Terri sleeping in our room a few doors down the hall, everything in our room—even a mouse in one of the walls. The only things I couldn't see were the things in my grandfather's room.

My eyes were shut tight, but I could see or maybe just sense an outline of everything as well as its presence. Almost like X-ray vision but extremely enhanced. I sensed things around me that no ordinary human could see, feel, or hear. No colors except a faint, light blue that outlined all the objects. Every figure was very blurry and fuzzy. It was as if every atom of the universe became a part of me, as if I could control them all ...

I wondered what was happening. It was so strange, but it was also the best feeling ever. Adrenaline surged through my body, and I felt like the strongest person on earth. I felt I was changing but staying the same—all of it happening at once. I wondered if Livia felt this too.

I started to freak out in the dark because of what had happened the last time I was enveloped in it, so I tried to force myself out of it. I opened my eyes, and it was black at first, but my vision came back.

"What happened?" I asked.

"I remember my first time putting that thing on," Theo said with a chuckle.

"Please answer my question," I said flatly.

"What just happened to you was like Livia's fiery explosion. It was you and the amulet bonding. Some are more dangerous than others, as you now know. When you were in pitch-black, you were soaking in the power of the amulet and adapting to its new senses."

"Fair enough. Then what does it do?" I asked, getting a little antsy about that.

My grandfather held out a quarter. "Reach your arm out and have your palm face the coin." I did so. "Concentrate on its being and presence, then raise your arm a little."

I started to have a few guesses, and I got excited. I closed my eyes and sensed the quarter. I felt its round and flat shape. I could also sense its material. That was my kind of power.

I raised my arm, and what happened was exactly what I predicted. The quarter floated in the air. I opened my eyes to make sure my new senses weren't lying, and sure enough, there it was, slowly turning in the air.

Theo smiled. *"That's* what it does."

I let out a huge smile as I stared at the coin. It felt

awesome to have such powers. It even fit me perfectly. *Now I can help Livia carry wood to the tops of the trees!*

"Remember," he said, "the powers will be fun to mess around with, but there are two things you need to know. First, do not let anyone see them. You probably already know to hide them, but I am making sure. These families we have been working with for years trust us to not expose our secrets, and we trust them to do the same. Of course, you should show them to Livia, Terri, Emmett, and Zack, even Luna, but nobody else.

"Second, always remember that the bigger the object, the more energy it takes to move it. A quarter is effortless, and moving even a whole person takes little power, but don't try moving a huge boulder or anything heavier than a ton or two because you will have a high chance of passing out."

I nodded. I took note of two words he had said: *whole person.* I looked at him with excitement, and he must've read my mind. "Go on, try it," he said, almost as if I were a kid trying out a birthday toy. I closed my eyes. I focused on myself. I tried to feel every inch of my body. I imagined myself levitating a few feet. It worked. I felt the floor drop out from under me. I opened my eyes, and only air was below my feet. I would have hit the ceiling, but my new powers helped me sense where it was without even looking, so I didn't bonk my head.

I moved from side to side a bit just to get the feel of it. I laughed. The sensation of floating was so much fun. My grandfather watched me with concern in his eyes but a smile on his lips as I floated around. I felt weightless.

"You don't have to close your eyes to move an object," he said, "unless that is more comfortable or easier. Closing them is really only for trying to find something or to sense things you can't see."

"I can't believe I'm flying! Or that I can lift things effortlessly. I think I like these powers better than Livia's."

"I had a feeling this one would be your favorite," my grandfather said. "But remember, there are more out there, so be careful to choose who gets what amulet. Each will belong to only one person."

"Theo?"

"Yes, Jayce?"

"Where did these amulets come from?"

"Ahh. I remember this like it was yesterday. A long time ago, before you were born, your father and I created them with the help of our weapon designers and enchanters. We made only a handful, about seven, though I don't completely remember if that was the exact number. Only your father and I and five other trusted people used them, and for safety reasons, we had made them to be bound to only one being.

"Your father had made the aegris so they could easily be found as well as other important reasons. One day, though, almost two to three years ago, that shadow attacked us here, where all the amulets were for testing and training, as well as your father and me.

"We panicked. Everything was chaotic. We decided to hide the amulets in different parts of America to make them harder to find. I kept mine here since I knew I could protect it well. Your father hid both his and the aegris here for me to protect because he had to help somewhere else I cannot mention. Ever since we were attacked, the shadow has been going after them. I have heard the other families have started calling him Nightshade. His powers are very dangerous, and even just a hit in the head can make you ooze some of his black poison."

That reminded me Livia had told me about black liquid coming from my head after the first attack.

"He can take shape of anything, though we usually see him as a shadow, which is probably his primary form. Only a few times have we seen Nightshade in human form, so you were lucky to see that. What did he look like?"

"Scary." I tried to remember. "Most of his features matched his powers. He had dark hair and black eyes, and everything he wore seemed like shadows. I got to see it for only a few seconds before he lunged at us."

My grandfather nodded and stared at the floor. "Yes, that's what I remember too. It's Nightshade all right."

"Theo? We have one problem."

"What is it, Jayce?"

"Nightshade took the aegris. It's gone."

Theo pressed his lips together. "That's not good. You have to get it back no matter what. You can't go on the journey without it. For now, go to bed. We will talk to the others in the morning. If your sister is still awake, don't tell her anything. It's best it comes from me."

"Okay, but just a recap. The amulet eclipse happens on August … 24th?"

"August 27," he corrected.

"And it destroys the amulets. Nightshade, some shadow man, is going after some valuable object you aren't telling me about." I put a little sign of irritation in my voice to let him know I wanted in on that information. "He's making the eclipse happen because it's the only way to deactivate the amulets, which have the power to stop him. Right?"

"Right."

"You *think* there are seven amulets with different powers. And finally, this was all created by some collaboration of trusted families working with us to save the world, and for some reason, my generation is the most powerful. That's why you're sending us to stop him. This is the weirdest and most unbelievable conversation ever."

"But it's true. You have to trust me."

I did. It would be hard not to believe when half the stuff he was talking about had actually happened to me such as the amulets and Nightshade.

"Do not forget any of this. It is crucial information for your mission."

"Don't worry. I have it all up here," I said, tapping my skull.

Theo patted my back. "Get some sleep. Goodnight, Jayce."

"Goodnight," I said just as his door closed.

I snuck to my room and got into bed. I felt the amulet around my neck. I decided to keep it on just in case Terri saw it in the morning. I fidgeted before I fell asleep. I had another nightmare.

22

I was in a dark room. My amulet was giving off a faint glow. I looked around but saw nothing but darkness and the floor. The space around me and the floor seemed to have a tinge of red.

I walked around a bit, but there wasn't anywhere to go. I tried to feel for a wall or object, maybe a person, for a few minutes, but no luck. I just stood there. "What kind of dream is this?" I asked aloud, hoping for something in the dream to respond.

Making any noise turned out to be a bad idea. A ring of fire about ten feet in diameter erupted around me. I jumped, startled. I turned around. I was surrounded. The flames were up to the ceiling. I saw no way out of the circle of death.

I had nothing to douse the flames with or any way of getting over them. I stayed in the middle, where it was coolest, but I started sweating and breathing heavily in the heat. *What's happening?* I called out my friends' names. If I were in a dream, it was very real. I tried to get close to the flames to spot any exit, but I didn't have the other amulet, so I wasn't resistant to fire. The heat was scorching me. The only noises I could hear were the flames crackling and my voice. I was going nuts.

After a few more painfully slow minutes, I heard footsteps. I turned. A figure stepped through the inferno. "Livia!" I ran to her, but I stopped when she raised a blazing hand. Her irises were pure red. Her face was brutal and deadly serious. She almost had an angry and murderous look in her eyes. I was confused. "Livia?" I put my hands up in front of me and backed up a few steps, trying not to show any aggression. The figure didn't seem like Livia.

Once I was on the other side of the ring, which was still not far at all, a shadow formed behind her and took a human shape, the same man I'd seen before I got stuck in the darkness. I wanted to lunge at him, injure him, kill him somehow. But I couldn't. He was standing behind Livia, who still had her deadly stare locked on me.

The man started to speak, but instead of the sound coming from his mouth, it rang inside my head. *This is what will happen if you try to defeat me.* His whispering sent chills up my spine in spite of the heat. *Your friends and loved ones will turn on you. You will die a slow death with no legacy. No one will remember you.*

"You're lying!" I shouted. I couldn't take my eyes off Livia. I couldn't believe she was staring at me with such hate. She looked as though she would kill me if she could. I couldn't show any weakness. "They would never leave my side! You're just trying to deceive me. They would *never* join you!" I yelled at him with hate.

The man nodded at Livia, who started forming a fireball in her hands. It rapidly grew from baseball size to basketball size.

Okay then. Have it your way. Now you will suffer. Watch her kill you right now, I heard. I looked at Livia with pleading eyes. "Livia, please, no," I said quietly.

"Sorry, Jayce." Her tone was flat in spite of her hateful look. She launched the fireball at me. Flames splattered all over my chest.

I woke up screaming.

Terri ran over. "Jayce, you okay?"

I tried to slow my breathing. I swallowed. "Yeah, I think I'm fine. Just a nightmare."

"It must have been a bad one. I've never heard you scream in your sleep like that."

She crept downstairs to get a bottle of water from a vending machine in the shop. My throat was super dry, and my voice was scratchy.

She came up with two waters and handed me one. I gulped down.

"Need anything else?"

"No. Thanks for the water."

"No problem. See you in the morning."

"Have a good sleep," I said. I suddenly remembered the amulet. It had fallen underneath my shirt, so Terri hadn't seen it. I was relieved.

We got back into our beds, but she was looking at me, concerned.

I smiled. "Don't worry. I'll be fine."

She gave me a weary smile and closed her eyes. I did the same.

But I tossed and turned trying to get the image of Livia's deadly stare and her fireball out of my mind. It had seemed so unreal, yet it had also seemed so real. After staring at the ceiling for a long time, I drifted off. No more nightmares. At least that night.

23

The next morning, I found my grandfather in the shop helping a woman figure out what size T-shirt to buy.

"Should I get an adult large, my regular size, or are these T-shirts really big? Should I get an adult medium?" she asked.

"I would just get the large," he said. "If it doesn't fit, you can exchange it."

She went with his offer and walked to the cash register. I went up to him.

"So Theo, what's my job today?" I asked, trying to keep it casual just in case last night had been a dream. But I knew it hadn't been.

"I need to get your sister and all your friends. Even Luna, even though she already knows about it," he said, shuffling some shirts on a rack.

"Wait. Who else knows?" I asked, leaning in.

"Everyone in her family as well as everybody in the other families. The only reason we hadn't told you and Terri was because you were the ones most in danger and we knew you weren't ready then. But now you are." He whispered the last few words because someone was walking by.

"Do you think you could help us with some training before we leave to find the amulets?" I whispered.

"Of course. But once you leave, you'll have to work with the amulets yourself."

I nodded and went upstairs for Terri. I walked down the hallway and thought, *Why has he forbidden us to go in his room? There's nothing bad he could possibly be hiding.* I looked behind me. No one was around. I closed my eyes and saw Terri asleep and my grandfather downstairs helping people. I reached for the doorknob. A little voice in my head said, *Don't. Not now.* I shook my head. I thought, *Another time. A safer time. Theo will be suspicious if I take too long waking Terri up.* I pushed the temptation away and walked to our room.

Terri's head was under her covers. I tried to shake her awake, but she just threw off most of her covers and rolled over, groaning. After other gentle attempts, I whacked her with her pillow.

She sat up and groaned. "Ugh, what?" She rubbed her halfway-closed eyes. Terri wasn't what you'd call a morning person.

"Terri, get dressed. Theo needs to have an important talk with us and our friends."

She came to. "You talked to him? What did he say?"

"Exactly what he's going to tell you today. You'll find out."

Her eyes lit up. She jumped out of bed, something I'd rarely seen her do. I walked downstairs as she got dressed.

"I woke her up and told her you had something important to tell us all, Theo. That got her attention. She'll be down soon. I'll get the others."

He thanked me as I walked out the door. I tried to sense where everyone was, but my powers didn't go that far. I didn't know which hotel rooms they stayed in, but it wasn't super early, so I thought at least one of them would be up and about.

Zack, Emmett, and Luna were at the restaurant, and I saw Livia coming out of the hotel. When we were gathered at the table, I told them my grandfather needed to explain some things to us. I saw Luna's eyes meet mine. She raised her eyebrows and mouthed, *"Do you mean the CPA?"* I gave a slight nod when no one was looking.

We headed out toward the shop; my grandfather met us halfway across the field and told us to follow him to the hotel.

As we were walking, Livia took my hand and whispered, "What's going on? Did you talk to him?"

I paused, deciding what to say. She raised her eyebrows. I said, "Don't worry. He'll explain everything."

Theo led us to a small meeting room. We took seats. My grandfather closed the door and launched right in.

"I understand you have found some strange things on this island such as the aegris and that amulet," he said, pointing to Livia's neck. She pulled out the amulet and looked at my grandfather in a weird way. He nodded. "Well, it's true. The island isn't normal. I promise to answer your questions as best I can."

He told them what he had told me the night before, and my friends asked a million questions. They were as dumbfounded as I was at the whole thing.

He mentioned the other amulet and said he had given it to me. I pulled it out of my shirt, and they started at it slack-jawed. He asked me to demonstrate my powers. They of course were blown away when they saw me flying. I even lifted Terri as a joke, but she got scared. I put her down.

He told everyone about the CPA, the amulet eclipse, my father, and where the amulets had come from. The only thing he didn't tell them that he had told me was about Luna getting carried away at times. He mentioned Luna knowing about it, and Emmett looked at her. He was confused. She just nodded.

"Zack, Livia, and Emmett, you are the three rare people who have just as much power though you aren't in the families. After we found out you had the same abilities as we do, we sought you out. I asked your parents to send you here a year ago, and they know everything about it too."

I turned to Livia. She shrugged. "It's true. He asked me to come here, but I thought it was because they were looking for summer help."

When my grandfather finished, Zack asked something I hadn't thought of before. "What powers do the other amulets have?"

"Oh," Theo said, "with my old mind, I remember only two others, but I'll let you find out what power they hold."

Zack leaned back in his chair and folded his arms, his lips tightly pressed together.

"I have one question," I blurted out without thinking. *Ugh, why did I say that? I should've asked this later.* Everyone turned to me. I had to follow through. "I want to know how Emmett knew Luna before she came here."

"My mom has worked here since I was seven," Emmett said. "Long before you and Terri came, when I was eleven, Luna's family visited here, and I met her."

"My family was coming here to train with your grand-father," Luna told me. "But he didn't know that until now."

"We became friends," Emmett said, "and since you guys came, I guess her family wanted to come here too. We've been great friends for years now, so I'm surprised she's known about this all along." He gave Luna a look that said he was ticked off about her not telling him.

She shrugged it off. "I wasn't supposed to tell anyone, or I'd be punished. What we're dealing with here is super confidential. If this were to become public knowledge, the government would be on us after an hour at most."

There was a pause. My grandfather said, "Okay. These next few weeks, I will be giving some of you weapons and helping you train with them until you find more amulets to fight with. I will help Jayce and Livia with their powers though I assume Livia has already gotten the hang of hers."

We nodded.

"Does anyone have any skill with a certain weapon?" Theo asked.

"I used to take archery lessons," Emmett said, "and I'm still pretty good at it."

"How good?"

"I can hit a bulls-eye if I try hard," Emmett replied.

"Perfect. Anyone else?" My grandfather looked around the table.

"I'm really quick with a knife thanks to my dad," Luna said a little louder than usual.

"Great. Terri and Zack, tomorrow, we can give you other weapons to see which one fits you best," Theo said. "We can also get Luna's dad to enchant a few since he came with her."

"Wait a second," I said. Theo looked at me. "Where are we going to train? In the same spot where Livia and I did?"

He smiled. "I am no amateur concerning such matters. I have a great place to train."

"Where?" I asked.

"Want to start training today?" he asked with a smirk.

"Let's go," I said.

My grandfather beckoned us to follow him. He told Luna, "Find your father. He will assist us."

She ran up some stairs and was soon coming down with a man following her. He had blond hair in contrast with Luna's dark hair, but he had her piercing, bright-blue eyes. He was much taller than Luna. They looked nothing alike, but I assumed he was her dad.

"James," Theo said, "we need your help in training and enchanting. Would you mind?"

"Sure thing, Theo," James said. "Always happy to help new recruits."

"This is Zack, Livia, Terri, and Jayce," my grandfather said as he pointed to us one by one. "They are supposed to stop the amulet eclipse along with Emmett, whom you already know."

"You guys are in for a treat. You'll like training, though the first few days will be tough." He looked down at us, which made his height almost menacing.

"Come on, everyone," Theo said as he and James ushered us out.

We walked across the field and ended up at the shop.

"Where could we possibly train in the shop?" Zack asked, clearly unamused.

"Not *in* the shop," James said. He led us around to the back of the building to some locked cellar doors. "*Under* the shop."

My grandfather spun a combination lock back and forth, jiggled it a little, and pulled on the doors, which squeaked. We went down a few steps and entered a small room with just a few storage boxes. Two locked doors were at the end of the room. Theo started on one lock.

I decided to put my powers to use. "I have the other lock," I said. He nodded and continued to scroll through random symbols.

I closed my eyes and sensed the parts of the lock inside and out. I moved the parts and pieces around, sliding and twisting, until I thought it was unlocked and then made the metal loop push up. It worked. I laughed. "Hey! I'm getting the hang of this."

Once the other had opened, James pushed the doors open. We saw a small freight elevator, more of a platform attached to gears and cables and lit by a single bulb on the ceiling of the contraption.

We all squeezed on the platform. It began to descend. There were no walls to the platform, so we saw pipes and cables on the down. We descended through a thick layer of rock and dirt and then a layer of metal. The light swung back and forth as we went down. After a few more seconds of dropping, we stopped at some doors. They opened. We filed into a huge, dark room.

I heard a switch being flicked. Strips of huge lights flickered on one by one until the huge room was brightly illuminated.

I looked around the most amazing room I'd ever seen.

24

We were in what looked like a huge training facil-ity, big as a warehouse. It seemed like something I'd see only in a movie. But it was real life. I gasped as I looked around.

I saw ranges for archery and other weapons such as spears and throwing knifes. Dummies and targets, some hanging from the ceiling, were all over the gym. Ropes, weights, cargo nets, and rings were obviously meant for building strength, and an obstacle course suggested we'd train to build up our agility.

On one wall, long shelves and cabinets with glass doors held all sorts of weapons and fighting gear—from knives to armor to magical items, they had it all. I saw only a few guns.

On the opposite side of the room were doors with viewing windows next to them. As we walked by them, Theo told us what they were for. A few were secured target ranges for more-dangerous items, and one was an enchanting lab. Some were to test prototypes for new magical items, and the last one was my favorite.

It was different from the others; it was an empty, white

room, bigger than the others, with a headpiece hanging from a machine in the ceiling. We were told that it went over our eyes and generated a fighting scene we could customize. The machine moved around comfortably so it wouldn't get in our way while fighting. If you got hit, you lost. The headpiece came off, and you started over. The machine also projected the fighting scene in 3-D around the player and on the walls so the viewers could see what the fighter was seeing as well as doing.

James did an easy fighting scene with his long knife just to demonstrate how it worked. I'd never seen such quick and strong fighting skills; my friends and I were fascinated. If you won, which he did easily, you'd get points added to your training statistics that would show up on a monitor. The highest level was 100, which Luna's dad had already reached in knife and agility skills, but it had taken him years to achieve that. The rest of his skills were either high or moderate. The big TV flashed names and stats. My friends and I had zeroes after our names, but Luna's statistics read between 35 and 40; she had been training since she was ten.

In one corner of the gym was a small ring for one-on-one combat. I saw Zack eyeing it. I knew he couldn't wait to wrestle someone. Anyone.

Without thinking, I flew to the ceiling as the others watched. I moved slowly around a ring hanging a little low, touched it, and flew up to some bars at the top of the roof that spanned the room. I floated in and out of obstacles in the air, in between them, examining them all. I looked around the room from high up and saw all the practice ranges neatly lined up. I saw extra dummies and targets piled in corners and a few ropes and weights.

"How long did it take to make all this?" I called down, awestruck at what I saw.

"Me, your dad, James, and a few others built all this. It took a while," my grandfather said. "James enchanted our shovels and other tools, so it didn't take long to dig the place out. But it took a while to build it all. We could get only limited amounts of material at a time. We used some on the gift shop so people wouldn't get suspicious. I also used the amulet, the one you are wearing, to carry heavy objects and put things together. It took a long time, but it paid off."

"How could you build something this big? Magic?" I asked.

"I told you we're different from others. Smarter, faster, stronger. It's in our DNA. I guess you could say it's something like magic, though I would say it wasn't. We make up the CPA. We can do almost anything," Theo explained. He turned to James. "It's been such a long time since I've been down here with you, James."

"It sure has, Theo. Remember when we were down here last? A long time ago ..." James and Theo carried on for a while. Zach and Emmett were wrestling in the ring, Livia was gazing longingly at a golden mace, and Luna was training on the archery range.

I touched down and watched Luna shoot. She wasn't the best, but most of her arrows hit the target. When she ran out of arrows, a machine pulled the arrows from the target. I figured the arrows found their way back to the dispenser where she would retrieve more and carry on with her shooting.

I decided to have a little fun. I grabbed three arrows from the container and went to the lane next to Luna's. I used my powers to raise the arrows above my head and point them at the target. I shot them at the bulls-eye at full speed, and they all hit it with a loud thud. The ends were sprouting from the center in different directions while the tips were touching in the middle.

Luna smirked. "Show off," she said jokingly.

I smiled and shrugged.

I hovered all around the training facility close to the ground. I tried to get the feel of it so I could do it without thinking, but that wasn't hard. I just had to think of where to go and I'd float there. The amulet did all the work; I only had to steer, no great drain on my energy. Picking up heavy things proved to be exhausting, though. I tried lifting a heavy weight to which ropes were tied. I lifted a three-hundred-pound dead weight only a few feet before I got too tired.

I ended up at the ranges for different weapons, where Zack was throwing knifes. He nodded in acknowledgement and continued to throw them at a dummy.

I scanned the dispensers behind him; they held bullets, throwing knifes, and other sharp weapons, darts, and even some spears. I took four spears to a throwing lane, put three down, and figured out the best way to throw the one I held. I threw it with all my might. When it started to dip in flight, I mentally bent its path toward the dummy. It was harder than I thought. The tip just grazed the dummy's shoulder.

"You were gripping it wrong," Zack said. "When you're throwing it like that, not even your powers can help it hit square in the center."

"How about you teach me how to do this?" I asked him in a cheeky tone.

"I don't know how to throw a spear, but I know you did it wrong. Throwing knifes is similar, and you completely missed even with your powers. It was obvious you were trying to use them. Theo already taught me how to use knifes before you came over, and turns out I'm pretty good at it."

Before I could think, he drew back his arm and flung a knife that hit his target square in the chest. Thunk. I nodded my approval and clapped.

"Well done, Zack!" My grandfather came over to pat him on the back. "Need any help with those, Jayce?" He pointed to my other spears.

I pursed my lips and nodded. He showed me how to hold the shaft correctly; I realized I had held it at the wrong spot, but I quickly learned the right way. Soon enough, I was throwing more accurately.

After a few more rounds of throwing, I looked at the TV and saw Zack's name in big, bold letters and a score of 6 in knife throwing.

"How did you get to that level so fast?" My eyes went wide.

He looked at his name and score; the readout turned to Livia's name and score. "I'm better at this than I thought I would be."

James walked over. "Everything all right over here?"

Zack and I nodded. "He's really good with knives," I said, jerking my thumb at Zack, who gave me a smile.

James went to a nearby screen and tapped it a few times. "Yes he is. Each of us has a weapon he or she is better at than others, but Zack's quick-learning skill is rare. Have you ever done this before?"

"Never," Zack said, "but I've always wanted to try it. I used to throw cards like this a lot, and I was good at it, so I thought maybe I'd be somewhat good at this too." He looked exhilarated.

"You're fantastic with those blades," James said. "Remember, the higher the level, the harder and longer it takes to reach the next one, so don't think you'll be getting to level twenty today." James smiled. "When you think you're ready, I'll be happy to make and enchant special knives for you unless you find another weapon you're more comfortable with."

"Yes sir," Zack said as James moved on. He faced me with a huge smile. "Dude, did you just hear that? I have a rare skill. This is the best day ever!"

I smiled and continued throwing spears. I started hitting a few more bulls-eyes than usual and was becoming proud of my growing skill. When I got tired, I walked over to a screen with many buttons, different ones for different options such as weapons, a map of the place, and a view of what was happening in the simulator. The last button was for names and stats. I clicked on the statistics button and scrolled down. Most were people I'd never heard of—Wilson, Powell, Wolf—but then I saw my older cousin's name, Annabelle, as well as her mother's name, Ava. I also saw my uncle, Michael, who had no kids; Annabelle's brother Dylan, and many others in my extended family.

I came to my name in the *J*s along with my dad's and someone named Jake. Before I clicked on my name, I decided to see my dad's stats.

He was good at spears; he was at level sixty-seven. He seemed to be particularly good with daggers and combat knifes, which I had seen a bunch of on a rack. He was at a strong level of ninety-six. I made a mental note to try them later; I figured I might be good with those too. His archery was only forty-two, and axes were at a low fifteen. But his strength level was a fantastic seventy-four.

I viewed my stats. My spear throwing was a five. *Not bad.* It wasn't far behind Zack's eight in knives, but he'd left a while ago, so I had been there much longer than he had.

Livia stopped me as I was walking to the agility course. "Training's over. It's going to be short today. Tomorrow will be much longer, and we'll get instructions on something new of our choice."

We headed to the elevator.

"What did you do?" I asked as I put my arm around her.

"I tried this amazing-looking mace on a moving dummy, and I was only okay at it. I can probably find something I'd be much better at. I also went into the special target range in that safe room to practice my fire powers. What about you?"

"Mostly just throwing spears. I got comfortable with that. I saw my dad's stats. He's good at throwing spears too, but he was the best with daggers and knives, so I'm going to try them tomorrow. This is fun, isn't it?" I smiled at her, and she replied with a grin and a nod.

We waited at the elevator with James. The others came from two paths that led through a maze of trails into different features of the gym. Once all of us were at the elevator, Theo turned off the lights and machines. The doors opened, and we all filed in. This time, instead of being in the back of the tightly packed platform, I was next to the doors. I saw my grandfather push a button, which was probably the floor that led to the surface. Below it was another button, obviously for the training gym. But there was another button ... *Could that be for another training facility? More testing rooms? Maybe other things they're hiding from us?* I decided not to ask about it. I stayed silent all the way up.

The cellar had an unappealing, musty smell I hadn't noticed before. I also caught a whiff of something disgusting, revolting, but unrecognizable. I had to hold my breath until I was in fresh air again.

Once we got out, the sun was setting. "Let's eat. I'm hungry," I announced. The others looked famished too.

James and Theo headed toward the hotel. They said they'd eat there and plan our training. The rest of us headed to the restaurant for buffet night. We got in line.

"Well," Emmett said, "what an interesting day."

Everybody nodded. We talked about what we'd trained on and what we were planning on doing soon, but we spoke in low voices whenever people came too close.

We got to the food—mountains of delicious sweet rolls, piles of juicy steaks, pots of steaming soups, pans of yummy vegetables, and good-looking, meaty pork chops.

I couldn't decide among so many options, so I ended up with a plate full of small portions of everything. Even Terri, a picky eater, found plenty to eat. Everyone else's plate was like mine except for Luna's. She'd collected only salad, rolls, a bowl of soup, and a few veggies.

"Vegetarian?" I asked.

She nodded.

We began to eat, which we did more than talk. The food was so good; the sweet rolls were heaven in my mouth, the steak was juicy, even the soup and vegetables were tasty, but the pork chop with gravy was the best.

"The cooks here deserve a raise," I said.

"Mmm-hmm," was the extent of their responses.

After our meal, we returned our trays and headed to our rooms. We all hugged each other goodnight.

My sister and I crept up to our room. I could sense my grandfather was asleep, so we were as quiet as we could be. Before going to bed, I went up the ladder in my closet to the roof for some peace and quiet and to write. I climbed over to my little sitting area and saw a folded note on my chair. No one else was up there. I put down my notepad, picked it up, and read.

Jayce,

I left this note here because I knew you were the only one who spent time up in this little resting spot. Please show it to Terri too. I want her to know I am able to contact you.

I see that your grandfather and James have begun to train you and your friends. You will be ready sooner than you think, for you are our most powerful generation. You must trust me and especially your grandfather more than anyone.

I cannot explain much right now except that you need to know I am watching you and that we will meet soon. I have waited about sixteen years to meet you. I had to leave right after you two were born. I promise I will watch over you and not let you get in harm's way until you can protect yourselves.

Remember, you and your friends are the most powerful beings in the world right now. You just have to learn just how to use that power.

See you soon,
John Hunter

25

I pounded on my grandfather's door with a firm fist. Terri was right behind me.

The door opened slightly. Theo poked his head out. "What is it?"

"Did you know about this?" I asked and shoved the note into his fatigued face.

He squinted and read it. "No. Where did you find that?" he asked sternly.

"On the roof. Sitting on my chair. No one was around."

"He must have sent it there."

"But how?"

"I do not know. Your father always stays where he is positioned."

"Then how are we supposed to meet him?" Terri asked.

My grandfather smiled. "We shall see. He is a smart man, just like you two. He probably figured out a way to get it here," he said. He put his hands on our shoulders. "I will send him a message to tell him we got his letter as well as how your training is going. You two can decide whether to show your friends the letter."

Terri's eyes grew huge. "Can *we* send our dad a message?"

"No." He was stern. "You cannot. It … it's too complicated to explain."

Terri and I exchanged confused looks.

"I know, I know. You're probably frustrated because you know so much yet there's still so much to learn. But please, bear with me. I promise everything will be explained soon." Theo sighed.

I got angry. "You're just going to leave us like this knowing we've been lied to all our lives? We *still* don't get a full explanation? You tell us barely anything about our dad when we've just learned he's *alive?* You expect us to go on an extremely dangerous mission and come out in one piece after training for only a few weeks?" My rage took over. I didn't care. I couldn't stand his holding back on me.

"Jayce, please, I know you two are frustrated, but now is really not the time to jump to conclu—"

"No! I don't care what you have to say! You're sending us on a suicide mission. There's no point in going. Do you even care about us?" I gave him an infuriated look.

Terri grabbed my arm. "Jayce, he's right. Maybe you should calm down."

I became even more furious. *My own sister turning against me?* "Stop it! You're just taking sides! Get off me!" I yelled and flung her to the side. I was about to attack my grandfather when I heard a thud and a cry of pain. I saw Terri had hit the wall. She was slumped on the ground and clutching her shoulder. "Terri! I'm so sorry! I didn't mean to."

She cringed. "No! Don't touch me. You've done

enough." She struggled to her feet and shuffled to Theo for protection. Their looks told me something was wrong. I crouched, full of guilt. We were silent.

Then came the pain in my head. It felt like someone was hammering a nail through my skull from the inside out. I grunted and pressed my temples with my palms. My fingers dug into my scalp.

My grandfather gasped, not knowing what to do. "Jayce, what is wrong?"

I couldn't tell him. The pain in my head was too fierce, far too much to be a simple headache. I felt liquid oozing from my head. It came from the cut that was still healing. It was warm, almost hot, and felt slimy, runny. It scared us all. I felt so much pain. I heard faint laughter in my mind. I blacked out.

During the next hour or so, I became conscious but faded into unconsciousness. I remembered my grandfather saying something to Terri, who had run out of the building holding her injured arm. I remembered bandages being wrapped around my head. Then nothing. Unconsciousness.

When I woke up, I was in what looked like a hospital bed, but the room's looks told me I wasn't in a hospital. Everything was mostly metal. Cabinets lined the walls, tables were on either side of me, and a window was next to a door as had been the case in the training rooms. I tried to prop myself up with some grunting, but something tugged at my arms. I discovered they'd been tethered to something behind the bed.

I heard some scuffling. I saw James bent over a screen, rubbing his chin. In a minute or two, a small panel slid out of the tablet. He put his thumb on it, which made me guess it was a scanner. It slid back into its slot. The light glowing on his face changed color, though I couldn't see what was on the screen.

I moved around on the bed some more. He turned to me. "You're awake. Great." He walked over, pulling the screen with him. It swung out on a metal arm attached to the wall. He was facing me; I could see only the back of the screen.

"Wha ... what happened?" My voice was quiet and scratchy as if I hadn't used it in a while.

"According to your grandfather, you collapsed and blacked out. By the time I got there, a black substance was all over your head. I brought you here, a room in the back of the training area. It's a hidden hallway for different things like this. I patched you up, cleaned your scalp, and let you rest. During your sleep, you started thrashing around, so we restrained you. You finally stopped once we fixed you up and cured you. This is the first time you've woken up in days. It's Friday."

Friday? Before I'd blacked out, it was Tuesday. *That means it's June 23. August 27 is the deadline. We have only two months.*

James tapped a few more times on the pad. "Our theory is that when you got hit by Nightshade, he infected your head with this strange substance." He held up a beaker of dark, strange liquid. It was like looking into a void. "And he decided to use it against you at that moment. We also think it's why you suddenly turned so angry."

Theo appeared in the doorway. "I think you were already a little irritated at Terri and me, but your mood changed dramatically. We think that's when Nightshade took control of your mind. When Terri came close, he made his move and took over your mind just for a second, but that was all he needed. Once Terri had been hit, he left you alone. The substance caused the pain in your head, which took over your mind. I know you well enough that you would never do anything to hurt Terri no matter what. Luckily, we were able to extract all of it from you so it can no longer do any harm."

"Is Terri okay?" I asked.

"She's fine, She has a dislocated shoulder though. You probably shoved her harder than you thought. Your amulet probably helped with the push."

I looked down. My amulet wasn't there.

"Can I see her?" I pleaded.

"Maybe you should give it one more day of rest," James said, which probably was his way of saying no. "But I can send in the others."

"Please."

James and Theo walked out, and in a few minutes, Livia, Zack, and Emmett came in.

"She okay?" I asked. I knew they would tell me the truth.

"She's fine," Zack said.

"But she's on some pain medication, and I don't think she wants to see you," Livia said as she sat on my bed.

"You guys know I didn't mean to hurt her, right? I'm no psycho."

Emmett put up a calming hand. "Don't worry. James told us everything. And they have great medicine here, so you guys will be good as new in a few days."

"Is Terri's shoulder back to normal?"

"Theo and James were too busy with you, a more serious case," Zack said, "so Terri had no one to pop her shoulder back in. My dad's a doctor, and I learned a bunch watching him with patients. So yes, I fixed her shoulder, but her arm's in a sling."

James poked his head through the door. "Emmett, have you seen Luna?"

"Not in a while, why?"

"I just had to ask her a few things. Tell her I want to talk to her if you see her."

Luna? Missing again? Oh no. That can't be good.

James continued. "Zack, we need you in Terri's room to check her shoulder."

"All right. Emmett, come help. See you later, Jayce."

Emmett and Zack left. Livia asked, "You okay? I was so worried when you were still unconscious." She patted my head.

"I'm fine. Just a bad headache and some fatigue."

Livia looked at me with concern. She leaned over and planted a kiss on my lips. She stood and walked to the door. She stopped and smiled. "I'll check on you later. Feel better soon."

I didn't sleep that night at all. My pain and my guilt kept me awake, and even some sleeping medicine didn't work. I watched people walk past my window. I saw my grandfather, James, my friends on occasion, and a few people I didn't know, probably recruits. The only light came through the window.

I wanted to get up and move, but the people in the

hallway would see me. And I was still bound. My wrists had been rubbed raw. *Had I thrashed around that much? Probably the liquid in my head or a terrible dream I can't remember.*

I closed my eyes, but it was no use. I was wide awake. I opened my eyes for the thousandth time and saw Terri watching me through the window. She was expressionless. Her arm was indeed in a sling. I stared at her, not knowing what to do or say. Smiling would have been strange. I tried to sense her thoughts but could discern very little, and that was cloudy. All I could do was look at her.

She blew on the glass until there was a thin layer of mist. She wrote "KH'V FRPLQJ IRU BRX" on the glass. And then she was gone.

I lay down and tried to think about what I'd just seen. Was she checking on me? Was she even allowed to go outside her room? Probably not. Or was she even real? I might've been too tired and was seeing things. And what did those letters mean? I was starting to freak out a little, so I tried to convince myself I was dreaming though I was sure I wasn't.

I closed my eyes and willed myself to sleep. After half an hour, my body gave in.

26

The next morning, James visited me. He was
holding a clipboard, twirling a pencil, and humming a
soothing lullaby I'd never heard before. "Well, you seem
almost cured," he said. "You healed a lot while you were
unconscious and even more after you woke up."

"Great! I can finally go somewhere. But I have a
question."

"Hmm?"

"Is Terri allowed to leave her room?"

"No, but she isn't tied down like you are. By the way,
I'm permitted to take off the restraints." He bent down
and fumbled with some knots out of my reach.

"You sure? I thought I saw her last night outside my
window," I said.

James stood. My hands were once again free.

"Really? I could've sworn she was in her bed the
whole time last night," he said, clearly puzzled. But then
he sighed in relief and put a hand on his forehead. "Oh,
right. I forgot to tell you. Though the medication works
well with healing, your mind might see some crazy things,
hallucinations."

"I could've sworn she was real. She wrote something on the window."

James laughed. "Okay, I'll ask her. There's a chance it was real, but I think we should cut your medication in half."

"But are you *sure* she didn't come out of her room?"

"Jayce, it's fine. She can't leave her room. We lock her door from the outside at night."

I wasn't sure what had just happened. James completely dismissed my concerns as just illusions caused by my medicine. I swore I'd seen her by the window. I didn't know what was going on, but I knew something was up even if James doubted me.

I had checkups every thirty minutes; my stomach and head were poked, and that hurt. I was fed some sort of yellow mush every once in a while that I think was supposed to be some kind of chicken, maybe corn. Occasionally, my friends visited, but never Terri, which was distressing. I worried about her, but I also worried about our mission. I had to get back to training, quit wasting time.

I was allowed to walk up and down the hall. The rooms on either side of mine were empty. Terri's room was probably deeper in this seemingly eternal labyrinth of metal and technology.

I tried to sneak around a few times, but James or Theo or even someone volunteering to help would catch me and I'd be sent back to my room. They must have been watching me with cameras.

I got better and better. One day, I had terrible headaches, but I was generally less dizzy and was able to walk the hall without bumping into walls. I was determined to show them I was fine.

After countless attempts to convince them to let me go, I was finally going up the elevator and out of the cellar. When I emerged, the smell of fresh air had never been sweeter. Feeling the warmth of the sun was luxurious. I'd received my amulet, and I was just about to shoot up in the air in happiness when I realized there were people around.

So I ran. Across the field, into the trail, all the way to the spot where the cave was. I flew up as high as I could without going above the trees, afraid someone would see me. I floated around doing turns and flips. I felt so free with the wind under my feet and the ground way below. Once I had gotten all the flying time I needed, I wandered to the trail and back to the field.

I saw Zack talking to Emmett, so I jogged over to them. "Hey guys, they finally let me go!"

"Oh, hey, Jayce. That's great," Zack said. "Terri is out too."

Terri! I had to see her but decided to give it a little more time especially after what had happened the night before.

"What changed while I was gone, anything?" I asked.

"Nothing much," Emmett said. "Except that training got much harder."

"Mmm, wonderful," I replied flatly.

"I'm at level twelve in knife throwing and level nine in shuriken," Zack said with a smile. "Took me a while to get it, though. James is almost done enchanting some special knives for me."

"I'm a seven in archery and five in sword fighting. I'm terrible at knife throwing. I never even got close to my target. I hit Zack's instead," Emmett said and guffawed.

"Do we have training today? Am I allowed to go?" I asked.

"Yes and yes. Theo told us today," Emmett said. "Glad you're back."

"Trust me, I am too. Is it lunchtime yet?"

I'd endured almost two dreadful weeks of hospital food. I ordered two tacos with every topping the restaurant offered and was in heaven. I finished them before Emmett had made a dent in his salad.

"I was hungrier than I thought." I burped, and we all laughed.

Zack looked over my shoulder and smiled. I turned and saw my sister walking toward us. She was no longer wearing a sling, but she seemed overprotective of her arm; she was avoiding walls and people and holding it close to her.

She sat with us. I kept quiet but tried to say everything to her with my eyes.

"Hi," Terri said.

"Hey," I said but had no idea what to say after that.

An awkward silence.

"You okay?" I asked her, hoping she wasn't afraid of me.

"Yeah, but James said to take it easy. They also told me about the stuff that took over your head."

She looked calm. I tried to sense what she was thinking. I hoped our little trick would still work. It did. I saw the same feeling that was outside her. She really was fine.

It was as if she'd read my mind too. "I told you I'm fine. I'm not scared of you, honest."

We both smiled.

"Hungry?" Zack asked. "I can get you something."

"No thanks. I already ate."

"Where's Livia?" I asked, aching to see her.

"Hmm, where did I see her last?" Emmett mumbled to himself. "Sorry, no clue."

I looked at Zack. He just shrugged. I let out a sigh. I stood up and left, knowing where I should look for her first.

I walked down the path in the forest, looking up every now and then to see if Livia was up there. In five minutes, I was underneath the huge oak tree where I had first met her, but she wasn't there. I was exasperated. I slumped against the trunk and closed my eyes.

I felt the presence of another being near me.

"Looking for me?" she asked. I knew she had a smirk on her face. Hearing her voice made me smile. I opened my eyes and saw her standing on a branch a few feet above me, leaning against the trunk. She was beautiful. She had on worn jeans. Her hair was pulled back in a high ponytail with a bright-blue scrunchie. "I knew you'd come here," she said.

I flew up to her and embraced her. I kissed her. When she pulled away, she looked at me fondly. "I've missed you so much."

"I've missed you too." I pulled her into another long hug.

We sat in the tree talking and holding hands for an hour. I asked her about training, her powers, and what had been going on around the island.

"We're going to learn sword fighting as soon as you and Terri come back. They said even though we could fight with weapons of our choice, it's always good to learn to fight with swords since they're the most basic. Turns out, after some practice, I'm pretty good with a mace."

"Anything else new?"

She shrugged. "Not much."

I considered telling her about that night in the hospital. I wasn't sure if she would scoff at my concerns as James had or if she'd listen.

"Jayce, something wrong?" Livia must have seen the confusion in my eyes.

I glanced at her. "Hmm? Oh no. I'm fine," I said without thinking. I guessed I wouldn't tell her until I thought it was crucial. At the moment, Terri's message didn't mean anything, just some garbled text on a window. I still wasn't sure it had actually happened. Livia gave me a concerned smile. She stood on the branch and began to ascend. I followed.

About halfway up, she stopped. "What are we doing up here?" I asked.

"I need to show you something. Follow me."

Livia hopped onto a branch from a different tree, and I flew to her; I was excited to have my powers back.

I looked down. I'd never been afraid of heights, though flying was different from what I thought it would be like. I used to think it would feel like swimming except in air rather than water, but it felt as natural as walking. I could feel the air beneath me, but instead of feeling carried, I felt as if I were simply floating in space with the air supporting me but allowing me to move wherever I wanted.

I heard a small branch snap as she started to climb down. "Come on."

I followed Livia to the ground. We ended up in an open area, the same place we'd found the cave.

"What are we doing here?"

"The other day, I came here to check out the cave, but it took me a while to find the tree." She walked over to where the fake branch had been. To my dismay, it was no longer there. In fact, the whole tree was gone except for a sad stump.

"Where's the tree?"

"No idea," Livia said. "I was walking this way a few days ago and saw it was gone."

"But what about the cave?" I asked.

"Don't know about that either." She pursed her lips.

I closed my eyes and fell into darkness, feeling the essence of everything around me. I tried to sense under the ground, deep in the soil and rocks. I searched for the cave's entrance, but all I could sense was a huge boulder that had taken its place. I came out of my darkness and shook my head. "It's just a boulder. There's no cave anymore."

Livia frowned. "This doesn't make any sense. Nightshade must have done this. There might've been something in there."

"We need to tell the others."

We ran to the field and saw Zack and Emmett walking away from what seemed to have been a quick soccer game with some older kids.

"Hey guys, perfect timing," Emmett said. "We start training in thirty minutes."

"Emmett, listen," I said. "The cave is gone. Livia and I just checked. We think Nightshade destroyed it, or disabled it—we don't know. The point is it's gone."

"First the aegris and now the cave. What's next? Do you think he can steal the amulets too?" Emmett asked.

"I don't think so, but we should keep an eye on them. Livia and I are always wearing them, so it would be hard to steal them."

Emmett motioned Zack over. "Zack, the cave's gone."

"Oh well, that's just *perfect*," Zack said, throwing his hands up. "Real nice. What are we gonna do now? It won't be long until one of *us* gets taken away."

The thought of that made me shudder. *Could Nightshade really take one of us? What if he took me?* I pushed the idea to the back of my mind and shook my head. "Where are Terri and Luna?" I asked.

"They had to clean up the shop," Emmett said. "I'll get them." He ran across the field much faster than usual.

Zack, Livia, and I discussed our plans until Emmett came back with Terri and Luna. We told them what had happened, and we stood in silence.

"What now?"

I thought Luna had asked that, but I wasn't sure. I was staring at the ground thinking hard.

"I know," Zack said sternly. "We continue our training, we work hard, and we fight back before ... before *it* can take anything else away."

"But we need more answers," Terri said.

"Terri's right," Livia declared. "Right now, we know so little! Neither Theo nor James is telling us anything, and we're just getting more questions than answers. Like *you!*" Livia jabbed a finger at Luna. "Why do you have to be so *mysterious*? We barely know anything about you. You didn't feel the mist in the cave, you haven't told us anything about yourself, and you've barely said anything. We don't even know where you are most of the time!"

Luna backed up a step. "Livia, please, don't get mad. It's complicated, all right? I can't tell anyon—"

"You can tell us," Livia said. "Why didn't you test out the mist? Would it have hurt you? Do you know something we don't? What are you hiding? No more excuses!"

Luna backed up even more; terror was in her eyes. I looked closer and saw they were slowly changing from bright, vibrant blue to black.

"Please, don't do this, just back away ..."

No one knew what to do. We just watched.

"You *do* know something. Tell us! Why aren't we getting any answers?" Livia was getting angrier.

I put my arm on her. She was warm. "Livia, calm down, all right?"

"No! She's hiding something! Give us a straight answer!"

Luna glanced at her hands, looked at us wide-eyed, and ran off.

"Luna! Wait!" Emmett yelled.

"Go away! It's best for you guys!" Luna shouted over her shoulder. "Just leave me alone!" She disappeared into the woods.

Emmett glared at Livia. "Look what you did!" He chased after Luna.

Livia took a deep breath and cooled down. "I don't know what's going on. I guess I want answers is all.

Theo and James aren't talking to us even though they're pretty much using us to save the world. I guess I've finally snapped. Come on, let's find her."

We ran after Luna and Emmett.

"Luna!" he yelled. "Come back! Please, we need to talk! We're your friends. You know that! Livia just went a little crazy for a moment."

"Hey!" Livia shouted as she caught up to him. She shot him an irritated look.

"Sorry, but it's true," he said, raising his hands in defense.

"You're right. This is all my fault. I'm the cause of this. I lashed out when there was no need to. I'm fifteen. I should be able to control myself."

"Livia, it's okay," I said. "We'll catch up to her and you can apologize. We need to find her and get some answers."

"Come on everyone, move!" Emmett said between breaths. "I don't want to lose her!" He sped up.

We got to the small, open area and looked in all directions. The sun was casting shadows across the ground.

I felt chilled and looked at my feet. I saw a thick carpet of swirling darkness on the ground, a black fog covering my feet. The others noticed and started picking their feet up, though there was no spot the fog didn't reach.

"Nightshade," I whispered.

"Wrong," said a voice from what seemed like everywhere. We glanced around but saw no one.

Luna stepped out from under the shadow of a tree as if materializing out of nothing. "It's me. I took down the cave. I created this darkness." She spoke confidently but dejectedly.

"How?" I asked.

"Are you on Nightshade's side? Are you *helping* him?" Zack asked. He sounded scared but fierce; it was the angriest I'd seen him. "Livia felt bad after she yelled at you, but if you're helping Nightshade, we'll *fight* you if we have to."

"Zach, chill out," I said. Emmett and I grabbed him to keep him from doing anything stupid.

"Get back! *Run!*" Luna yelled. She opened her eyes wider. They were dark but glowing. The fog started to rise. I didn't feel anything, but the others except for Terri were groaning in pain.

"You have to get out of here," she shouted over the moans. "It's dangerous to be near me!" But she didn't sound threatening. She sounded scared.

Something clicked. Maybe from the feel of the fog or the sense I got, but my mind had put two and two together. *Of course!* "It's like the cave fog," I muttered. That was why the foggy carpet didn't affect Terri and me.

"Get *away!*" Luna screamed. The fog receded into the ground slowly.

"Luna, what's going on?" Emmett asked while grunting in pain. "Are you working with Nightshade? Why won't you tell us the truth?" He was tearing up. He had a distressed tone in his voice.

Looking more vulnerable and pitiful than ever, Luna bit her lip. A few tears rolled down her cheeks as she shook her head. "A few years ago, when Nightshade attacked the island in an attempt to get the amulets, I was there. He injured many people, but I was the only one struck directly by him. Everyone thought I'd die. Instead, he gave me some of his powers. They're a burden. I can't control

them. I don't know how to make them stop. All my efforts
to calm this eternal curse have been in vain. Sometimes, I
hear him in my head. He tells me that I'm destined to work
with him sooner or later, that this power will eventually
consume me. I don't know whom I can trust. Sometimes,
I don't feel like myself. Sometimes, I feel like *hurting* people." She exhaled as more tears came down. The fog was
nearly gone.

"I get a strange urge, and during these brief moments,
I don't know who I am anymore. I feel evil, ghostly. One
time, my dad videoed my powers taking over me. It was
shocking to watch myself turn into what Theo and my
father had been fighting for years. I don't want to become
something horrible like Nightshade, but I've started to
have less and less power over my abilities."

She wiped her eyes. We didn't know what to do. She
smiled faintly. "I used to have long, beautiful, blond hair
like my dad. But when I was hit, it changed to this dark
color." Her smile faded.

"And the cave?" Terri asked.

"I took it down on purpose. It was dangerous. The
little power I had over myself was just enough for me do
it. Nightshade was going to have it collapse on the next
person to go in there. I saw it in one of my visions," Luna
said. By now the fog was gone.

"I ran away because I could feel the dark power gathering in my hands. I didn't want to hurt anyone. Whenever
I get too angry or scared, or if any of my emotions turn
on me, bad things happen to me and anyone nearby." She
shook her head and took a deep breath. She turned to

Livia. "I gave you answers. Happy now?" Her smile was as sad as before.

Livia paused. "I—I'm so sorry. I didn't know you'd been going through all that. I didn't mean to explode. I wanted answers, but I didn't stop to think about the consequences. I hope you can forgive me, Luna."

Luna nodded and whispered, "It's okay." She bit her lip again. She closed her eyes and sighed. "You're the only people I've ever told besides Dad about this. I was always too scared, I guess. Thank you for helping me get some of this off my shoulders." She opened her eyes. "Come on. Theo and my dad are expecting us for practice right after the shop closes."

She headed out of the clearing. The rest of us exchanged bewildered looks that asked, *How is she okay after spilling her entire, tragic backstory?*

"Wait!" Livia called out. Luna stopped. Livia tackled her with a hug. "I'm so sorry about all this," she said, tears in her eyes. "Can we still be friends?"

Luna chuckled. "Of course, Livia. I know you're frustrated, all right? I understand." She embraced Livia.

"Group hug!" Emmett yelled. We all glared at him. "Not the time? All right ..." He shuffled off as Luna smiled a bit while Livia stifled a giggle.

"But seriously, we should head to the shop if we want to get any training in. Just don't tell my dad or Theo I told you all this, all right?"

"All right," we replied.

We followed her all the way to the shop, wondering what this meant for us and our mission.

27

We were mostly quiet during the training ses-sion. All we did for the first part was watch Theo and James demonstrate swordplay. We learned that guns cannot be enchanted and are useless against the enemies we will be facing.

By the end of our lesson, we had learned Luna was by far the best at sword fighting, but I was close behind. Livia was the best with a mace, which Terri and I couldn't even swing around. Livia had great upper-body strength because of all the rock and tree climbing she'd done. She ran around the battlefield slashing down straw dummies as if they were nothing, and she did it so gracefully, effortlessly. I told Terri she looked like a swan on the battlefield, and she laughed.

Terri was amazing at throwing shuriken, ninja stars. I'd toss her into the air, and she would throw them at targets and land and roll on a mat. After days of practice, she could throw three at once and have them all hit the center of the same target. I couldn't imagine what Mom would say if she knew about this.

During all our training, I wondered how we'd never

known what great, inherent skills and unbelievable talents we had that simply needed developing.

Theo told us we were nearing the end of our training and the start of our journey. Everyone had the same mixed feelings—excitement and nervousness.

I'd been trying to find a way to confront Terri about the message she'd given me that night, but the time never came up. Eventually, I pretended I wanted to show her something in a testing room and just about had to drag her away from training. But once we were alone, I had no idea what to say.

"Jayce, why'd you bring me in here? It's obvious you didn't want to show me anything."

"Well ..." *How can I ask, "What did you write on my hospital window?" Yeah, right. Great conversation starter.* I wasn't even sure she'd been aware of it. "You remember when we were in the hospital?"

"Of course."

"I remember your writing something on the window. Random letters."

"Didn't you remember our code?"

It came to me. When we were little, we used to use the Caesar cipher all the time, one letter in code referring to another letter in the message. We each made little decoding wheels so we could code and decode messages to each other and not worry about their being understood if anyone intercepted them.

I pulled out my notebook and pen and flipped to a fresh page. I drew our cipher wheel from memory, scribbling down letters and counting spaces. Terri watched in awe as I worked quickly but diligently. I realized the note had read, "He's coming for you." I gazed at my sister, half-scared, half-confused.

"That night, I got a visit in my dreams," she said. "I was sitting at a table outside at night with Nightshade. He talked to me, but I didn't know if it was really him. He told me he was going to visit you next. When I woke up from the dream, my door was standing open, so I knew I had a way to warn you. Have you had any weird dreams lately?"

I hesitated. "No, I don't think so. I don't remember any dreams with him besides a few before you wrote that note on the window."

"Okay, be careful. Let's be honest from now on. We tell each other about all our dreams, got it?"

I nodded. She walked out. I tried to comprehend what the message meant. *"He's coming for you"? Why didn't I think of our code sooner? I must've been overthinking it.*

I walked back to training. I watched Terri and Zack sword fighting, but I was spacing out most of the time.

I was afraid to go to sleep that night, but I finally drifted off. When I did, Nightshade came. In my dream, my cheek was pressed against a cold surface. I sat up and looked around. I was in a huge parking lot with only a few cars scattered here and there. It was foggy and dark. I scanned the area for someone I knew would come.

"Come out. I know you're here." I tried to hide the fear in my voice. I felt something strange. Turning around, I faced my enemy. He was closer than I expected, only a few feet away, but his face was hidden in folds of darkness.

"What do you want?" I asked, my voice quavering.

It's not what I want, it's what you want, I heard his raspy, alien voice whisper in my mind.

The aegris! I thought, remembering my grandfather telling me to get it back.

Correct, Jayce. He had read my mind. *Perhaps we can ... work something out. Maybe a trade.*

"If I get the aegris, what do I have to give to you?" I gained some courage just by asking that.

Nothing for now. I'll give it to you. But know this, boy. You owe me something. I'll take my share later on.

Hmm. Theo did say to get it back no matter what, I thought.

Do we have a deal?

The voice was taunting me. A dark, ghostly hand reached out, tempting me to shake it. I debated the pros and cons though I didn't have much of a choice. I knew there was probably a catch, but this was the only offer I was afraid I'd get. I reached for his hand, which was rough, and shook it. I felt something strong pass between us. I stared into what should have been his eyes. All I could see was a swirl of darkness, but I sensed his cold stare. We froze.

I jolted awake. The clock read 8:27, a very unusual time for me to wake up. Terri was in the bathroom brushing her teeth. I rushed in. "Terri! I had the dream. We made a trade." I reached into my pocket and felt the smooth ring. I pulled it out and showed her.

She looked fearful. "What did you give to him in return?"

I shrugged. "Don't know yet. He said he'd take something later on."

"That worries me."

"I know, but what other choice did I have?"

I dressed and rushed to the shop, where I saw my grandfather opening up.

"Theo, I did it. I got it back." I showed him the aegris slyly so the staff member there couldn't see.

"Good work. I knew you could get it back."

I was surprised but relieved he didn't ask me how I had managed it. I was afraid of his reaction if he learned about the terms of the trade.

"You must give it to me tonight. I know I can trust you, but I don't want to lose it again. It would be safer locked up in my room until we need it," he said.

But when exactly will we need it? I wondered.

"Carry it around for the day but don't lose it. Put it in a pocket with a zipper, and don't let it come out."

I nodded.

"Training starts a little early today. We will engage in something special. Tell your friends, and be there right after lunch."

My friends and I got in the habit of gathering at the pole every day. I told them about the dream and the aegris but left out the deal part. I could sense Terri was nervous, but she didn't say anything. We all made guesses on what special thing we'd be doing in training that day: Fighting with a new weapon? Learning a new technique?

After doing a few jobs around the island, we ate delicious fried chicken and rolls with melted butter. I wondered how they could serve such good food considering it all had to be shipped in.

As we ate, I looked out at the sky. The clouds seemed a little lower than usual, soft and fluffy, faded gray, and a thousand different sizes. They fascinated me because I was seeing them from a new perspective. Not in a way a camera would capture them, not in a way an artist would paint them, but in a way only I could see them. The drifted slowly, almost seeming to stop. I realized that with my amulet, I was like the clouds—weightless, floating.

I was with my good friends and eating delicious food. In my reverie, I forgot about our mission, about Nightshade, about the dangers of finding the other amulets. It was nice to have a break from that even for just a few minutes. I enjoyed not having to think about the pressure we were under if even for just a short time. I was relaxed. *After our mission, life could be like this every summer. With our family being as smart as we are, I could maybe even quit school and stay here. Have a good life training and work-ing with my grandfather. I could stay with my friends. Every day could be like this. That would be nice.*

Livia noticed my blissful look and asked what I was thinking about. I told her I wasn't really thinking about anything. Sometimes, it's good to keep things for yourself to enjoy.

After lunch, we walked to the shop and snuck around the back as quickly as we could. Theo and James were waiting for us outside the elevator doors.

"Welcome to training again," James said. "We enter our next phase today."

"We will start you out by battling a little bit in the fighting ring," Theo said.

They led us to the battling zone and a rack of weap-ons. "You choose whom you will fight and who goes first." James motioned at the rack. "Choose any of these weap-ons, but don't take more than you need. We have quick, pain-relieving medicine, so don't be afraid to hurt your opponents a little. However, we can't grow any limbs back, so don't go crazy." He laughed to himself, though we weren't sure if we should laugh.

Theo chuckled. "Don't scare them, James. It's only their first time battling for real. We still need to toughen them up for their mission." He clapped once. "Let us commence the training, shall we?" He and James walked up some steps to a viewing platform.

Livia and Emmett started things out. She grabbed her golden mace, and Emmett grabbed an unusually long sword. Both had shields.

They slowly walked around in a circle eyeing each other. It reminded me of fighting scenes in movies. Livia struck first; she lunged forward with her mace and swung it down on Emmett. He blocked the strike with his shield and tried to swing low at her, but she dodged it. They took turns swinging and dodging back and forth, but it wasn't long before Emmett swung at Livia, missed, and was struck by her mace on his shoulder. The mace had dull studs rather than spikes, but her blow was sure to leave a huge bruise.

He grunted and stepped back. His sword arm was fine. He swung his sword. Livia dodged most of the swing but couldn't use her shield in time, and Emmett hit a little bit of her elbow. She gasped in pain and grabbed her arm.

"Stay strong. Don't back down. Come on now!" Theo's voice boomed around the training facility.

They fought a little longer with a few more grunts and noises of extra effort. At one point, they struck at the same time, and as their weapons clashed, the chain on Livia's mace wrapped around the sword. The two froze for an instant as if the clash had sent a paralyzing pulse through them. But Livia yanked her mace down and ripped the sword from Emmett's hands. She raised her mace but stopped when she heard, "Enough!"

James clapped. "Good fight. Shake hands. There you go. That was great, but remember to never stop fighting in the middle of a battle. You two were lucky you froze, but you might have to fight more-experienced opponents. Good job, though."

Terri and Luna were next. My sister grabbed a few shuriken and a thin sword, while Luna wielded a long dagger. Their fight went somewhat like Emmett's and Livia's. Back and forth, striking and swinging their weapons. Terri threw two shuriken at Luna, but both hit her shield with thuds. Most of the time it was Luna attacking. I could tell Luna was a tough opponent for Terri, but Terri had cut the tip of Luna's ear with a shuriken. After touching the blood coming from her ear, Luna struck fiercely at Terri, who swung and blocked, dodged and parried. Terri was holding her ground, but I could tell she was losing.

Though Terri tried to block Luna with her shield, Luna's dagger ended up at Terri's neck. They paused. Luna lowered her weapon. "Good fight," she said. They shook hands.

"Very good," Theo said. "Terri lost, but she wasn't injured. She receives a small victory for hitting Luna's ear."

It was down to Zack and me. Because he was bigger and stronger, I knew I'd have to rely on cunning and agility. He chose a few throwing knives as well as the sword Emmett had used. I decided on a short sword and strapped a spear to my shoulders as backup. I grabbed a shield for protection against throwing knives, but Zack didn't want a shield.

We stepped onto the stage and watched each other. I was afraid of being hurt, but I knew Zack could aim well with his knives so he wouldn't hit any vital areas on purpose.

I ran forward and struck at him, but his sword stopped me. He swung at the side, but I was able to dodge the blow. After a few more hits, Zack backed up and switched his sword to the other hand. He reached for a knife in his belt. I ducked behind my shield just before the knife hit it with a thump. I glanced up to see another projectile heading my way. It barely missed my head. I frantically thrust my sword to prevent Zack from throwing any more knives. He quickly dodged and switched his blade to the other hand.

He struck me much more powerfully than the last time, and I fell back. My shield went up for protection, but I could see his arm raised, a knife ready to throw. I breathed hard, knowing I had lost. But James and Theo were silent. *What are they doing? I'm going to lose and even get hurt.*

I closed my eyes for a second to calm down. I felt the amulet around my neck warm up. I gained a little more strength. I opened my eyes with a surge of energy. I rose, weapon pointed at Zack. I did someone no one was expecting, not even me. I dropped my shield though Zack still had two knives. I heard Emmett ask, "What's he doing?" Theo and James just watched.

I grabbed my spear with my other hand. Zack grinned. He threw the knife at my right side. As the spinning blade flew at me, the amulet grew warm. Without even thinking, I jumped into the air, up, up, higher than a normal jump, and with my amulet helping, I landed on the other side of Zack. He whirled around but was too late to grab his weapon. I lunged forward, smacked the blade out of his hands with extreme force, and pointed my weapons at him, blade across his neck, spear at his heart.

Zack's eyes went wide. He froze. He held his breath. I could sense Theo nodding behind me. I lowered my sword and spear, but I made a cut across his upper arm with my sword. "Just a little souvenir for you to remember this fight." I smiled.

He exhaled and inspected the gift I had given him.

Theo broke the silence. "That was one of the most entertaining fights I've seen in a long time. Good job."

"You two did well," James said. He came down with ointment for Zack. "Zack did well with knocking Jayce down, but Jayce came back and defeated him. Definitely a good fight."

I shook hands with Zack, who smiled, though I could tell from the competitive look in his eyes that he wanted to get me back. *I'm sure we'll get to fight again,* I thought.

"You are all ready for the next step," Theo announced. "Follow me."

He took us into one of the testing rooms "James?" Theo asked. James pressed some buttons on his tablet. A large panel in the wall slid open, and inside were throwing knives in a belt. "Zack, come." James unsheathed a knife that shimmered and glowed. "We have designed and enchanted these knives for you. Here's how they work."

Zack put on the knife belt. James threw the one he

had at a target and hit it squarely. We stared in silence, waiting for him to say something. But after a few seconds, the knife seemed to dissolve into nothing. The target was blank.

"Where did it go?" Zack asked.

James smiled and pointed at Zack's belt. The knife was in the formerly empty slot.

"No way!" I said.

"The knives are enchanted. They will appear back in your belt after they've hit a solid surface. We're not quite sure how it works, but we have a theory that the knife's atoms pull apart and get disorganized but reattach and realign themselves at the destination we set it to."

James grabbed another and threw it. Again, the same dissolving trick occurred. "This is officially the coolest day of my life," Zack said as he threw a few more.

"Terri," James said, "We've designed some shuriken the same way for you as well as an extra perk. They are much sharper than regular shuriken, but they won't hurt you when you touch them. We just need to get your finger-prints here." He motioned to a panel.

Once she scanned all her fingers, a new panel slid open, revealing her personalized shuriken, each with the same shimmering glow that Zack's knives had.

Terri grabbed one and lightly touched the edges.

"Be careful, however," James said. "They won't hurt you, but they will hurt anyone else. Badly."

She started to throw some.

"Livia is next," Theo said.

Livia's eyes lit up.

"We have noticed you have a liking for the mace, and

it was a little difficult deciding what to do with it, but we figured it out." Another panel slid open to reveal a shiny, glowing mace. James handed it to her. "Since you have the power of the fire amulet, we allowed the mace to catch on fire and be put out at your will, making your weapon twice as dangerous."

Livia smiled and backed up into the testing range. Her hand caught on fire, and less than a second later, her mace was engulfed in flames as well. The heat made me uncomfortable, but she was thrilled. She swung the mace around a few times and turned off the fire. Emmett, Luna, and I were anxious to learn about our weapons.

"Emmett," Theo said. Emmett rushed forward in excitement as Theo grabbed a bow and a quiver of arrows from behind another panel that slid open. "Sadly, we could not make your arrows reappear in your quiver because they are too big, but we were able to give them a different perk."

Emmett took the bow and inspected it. It didn't glow.

"Look at the arrows," Theo said. They were indeed shimmering. Some had blue fletching, some had red, and the rest were yellow. "The blue ones are ice arrows. They will immobilize whatever they hit. The red ones are fire arrows that will burst into flames when they pierce flesh. The yellow ones are regular arrows. The heads of the blue and red arrows have heat-detecting sensors that detect warm flesh. The arrows are extremely durable and reusable, so you most likely won't break any. The flame or ice effects wear off once they do not detect body heat, when they are out of the flesh. Sadly, you can't test them now since we have no heated target to practice on, but we guarantee they work."

I could tell Emmett was disappointed at that, but he was nonetheless happy with his new, deadly toy.

"Who's next?" Theo asked James, who tapped the screen.

"Luna."

A panel slid open, but we weren't expecting what we saw—a light-blue, glowing crystal.

Luna grabbed it. "What is this?"

"You'll love this." James smiled. "Flick your wrist."

"What?"

"As if you were casting a fishing line."

Luna flicked her wrist, and two daggers, one slightly longer than the other, sprouted on each side of the crystal. Her eyes lit up. "Whoa!" she whispered.

"We designed it specifically for you."

It was strange to see a father proud of his daughter getting her first lethal weapon.

"To make the daggers go away, flick your wrist again."

Luna flicked her wrist a few times, watching the daggers shoot out and shrink back into the crystal. She put it in her pocket. "It's perfect." She smiled.

I was next. The last slot was long. *A spear!* I hoped. That was exactly what the panel revealed after it slid open. I grasped the spear and felt tingling in my arm. It started emitting a faint blue light.

"For you, Jayce," Theo said, "we have given you an electrified spear. It will not zap you, only your enemies. You can throw it, thrust it, or stab with it. As long as it detects some fighting movement, it will daze or confuse or even electrocute what it comes in contact with."

I stepped into the range and threw the spear. It hit the target, and I saw an electrified pulse run through it. I walked down the range and pulled it out. "Wow!"

"That concludes our weapon handout," Theo said. "We hope you like them."

"That's all for today," James said. "Put your weapons on this rack by your names. We'll train with them tomorrow."

It was late in the afternoon when we got out. We ate near the back of the restaurant and talked about our new weapons. We were excited and couldn't wait for the next day, though no one wanted to think about using them in a real fight.

After dinner, Terri and I headed to the shop. I heard a little chirp. The red bird perched on my shoulder. "Hello there," I said softly. "Nice to see you again."

"Is this the little friend you've been talking about?" Terri asked. I nodded. "Let's give him a name," she said.

The bird tweeted with delight, "Ca-*lip*-so."

"Hey, that sounds like Calypso. I guess she's a girl. Let's name her that," I said. She started hopping on my shoulder. "You're a smart bird, aren't you? You aren't like any other." She cocked her head. "Where did you come from?" I asked.

Calypso twitched her head and peered at her little talons. It seemed she could understand me but couldn't quite answer. She jumped off and flew into the night.

"Good-bye, Calypso." Terri and I waved, which seemed

strange at first, but it somehow felt natural to say good-bye to this bird.

We reached the shop. Theo stopped me inside. "Do you still have the aegris?"

"Yes. Give me a sec." I pulled it out and looked through it. I prepared myself for the dreadful, rotted world, but instead, everything was the same. Nothing gray, nothing glowing. "It doesn't work anymore."

Theo grabbed it and looked through it. "You are correct. Nightshade must have disabled it so we couldn't use it to find the amulets. No matter, however, because this also serves another very important purpose for your journey. Thank you for getting it back."

I nodded, glad to not have to worry about carrying it around.

"Phase-two training starts tomorrow, so get some sleep." He patted my back as he always did, and I went to my room. As Terri went to bed, I went up for some alone time on the roof. I drew everyone's weapons in my notebook and wrote descriptions of each one. I wrote down my thoughts about the day as I usually did, and I wondered what our journey would be like. I wrote down what I thought the other amulets would be and even drew them.

I was so caught up in writing and drawing that I didn't realize how tired I was for a solid hour. Exhausted, I stumbled down through the trapdoor and threw myself into bed.

With one last look at my latest additions to my journal, I put it aside and fell asleep, luckily with no dreams.

28

When I woke up, I realized it was almost July. *Our training must be coming to an end. We have to start the journey soon.* I couldn't decide if I was exhilarated or terrified about that.

That morning, Emmett and I were to chop firewood. I was pleased; the labor would make me stronger. We grabbed some axes from the toolshed and walked to the woods.

"How long did you say you've been here?" I asked. I was carefully holding my axe with two hands, but he just let his swing from one arm, which scared me.

"Eight years. When I turn sixteen, it will be my ninth. This place is practically my home." He smiled. I knew he was happy there.

"By the way, we've known each other for so long, but I don't even know your birthday. When is it?"

"October fourteenth. What about you?"

"May twelfth. I turned fifteen last month."

"Good. I'm older than you." He smirked.

Once we thought that we had gotten to where we were

directed, we set up some logs lying around and started to chop them.

"I see that you and Livia have fallen for each other," he said.

I laughed. "Yeah, she's pretty amazing. What about you and Luna? You two seem tight."

Emmett shook his head and grinned a bit. "No, we aren't dating." He paused. "Well, I know I can trust you. But don't tell her. I ... I've secretly been in love with her for almost two years, but she doesn't love me. She thinks we're best friends, nothing more."

"Emmett, you're one of the coolest guys I've ever met, and at least you guys are best friends. I bet one day she'll feel the same way," I said, but I didn't really know what to say beyond that. I wasn't very good at that kind of stuff.

He tilted his head. "Ahh, it's okay. I've lived with it for two years, and even if she doesn't love me in that kind of way, I'm glad she's my friend."

I hoped Luna would treat him well. Emmett was one of the nicest guys I'd ever met, and there was no way Luna wouldn't fall for him eventually.

"We'll get through the mission together, all of us. When it's over, we can all live on the island, and I know you and Luna will stay very close." I thought the conversation was sweet, but at that point, I wanted to change the topic so I wouldn't say anything stupid. "You excited about our upgrades?"

"They're super. James told me they would put heated pads in the targets, so I finally get to try my new bow and arrows. How's your spear?"

"I can't wait to try it out more, but I'm worried about unintentionally shocking myself. I can be clumsy at times."

"We'll get used to our weapons eventually."

We laughed and then focused on our chopping.

Once the hour was up, we returned our axes to the shed, took the cart back to the wood, and got all the wood back in two trips. Proud of our accomplishment, we high-fived each other and walked to the restaurant for a drink as a reward.

It was a Monday, the day that staff had to pay for their meals. I had some cash my mom had given me, so I treated.

At the table, I asked, "Do you know what everyone else is doing?"

"I think Zack is in charge of the shop today, but that's all I know." He shrugged and gazed outside at the drizzle that had started. "Glad we finished chopping."

I took a long sip of my soda and looked at the clock above the door. "Training is in an hour. I'm excited."

"Me too," Emmett said with a nod.

I enjoyed spending some time with him since we hadn't gotten know each other that much.

The bell on the door rang. Livia walked in soaking wet. She ordered something, and I waved her over. "How was your job?"

"It wasn't great. I had to help out with the climbing ropes at the wall, and then it started raining." A man came up with her lemonade, and she thanked him. "What about you guys?"

"We had to chop firewood, and we had a fun conversation." I smiled at Emmett.

We talked and sipped our drinks and decided to go to training early. When the elevator doors opened, we saw James and Theo setting things up.

Terri and Luna arrived promptly, but Zack showed up a little late. "Customer trouble at the shop," he explained.

"Retrieve your weapons," Theo said and waved to the shelves.

I flew over to the rack, grabbed my spear, and activated it as I had been taught.

Emmett caught up. "Lucky. You're so much faster with that amulet."

I laughed.

We practiced in the ranges, the fighting arena, and even the room with the simulator. I was able to do some of the easy and medium ones, but I couldn't land a single blow on the fake people in the hard simulation. Everyone had trouble at first, but by the end of the first session, we'd gotten used to our custom weapons.

We had more chances to fight each other as long as we disabled our weapons' special abilities. Sometimes I won. Sometimes I lost. But based on Theo's and James's reports, I was very good in battle.

We fought, trained, worked out, and tried our best throughout the week. It was rough, but we pulled through. My friends and I improved every day. I achieved level eighteen in spears and sixteen in sword fighting. I was proud of my accomplishments as everyone else was about his or hers.

We'd have dinner together, and some nights, Livia and I would zipline and discuss the day. I'd write in my

notebook every night about new discoveries or ideas—
anything that came to mind.

We were nervous. Our training was coming to an
end. Our mission would start. But we were determined
to try our best. Though we did normal teenager things,
we trained secretly and hard for three hours every day.
We were warriors preparing for battle. After every training session, we talked about the mission—what to expect,
things that might happen, how to deal with certain situations, everything.

We spent one training session learning CPR and other
medical things in case one of us got hurt. Zack didn't have
much trouble picking that up since his dad was a doctor,
but the medical stuff confused me. They talked about
some of the medicine they would give us on our journey
and what each did.

We discussed what we would bring on our mission
and how to get more supplies. We learned all about our
SCDs, satellite communication devices, which James had
modified so we'd be able to communicate with him and
Theo from anywhere in case of emergencies and with each
other during our mission.

"Why don't we use phones?" Zack asked.

"Bah!" Theo exclaimed. "Phones are completely useless in this world compared to our technology. They run
out their batteries, so you need outlets to charge them.
They need Wi-Fi, good connections, on and on. In ad-
dition, you can easily be tracked when carrying phones.
These are solar powered and have backup batteries as
well. They won't power down for a long time. They have
built-in flashlights too."

Our SCDs were pretty cool, and they weren't that big. We could clip them to our belt loops.

"Don't use them too much. Nightshade might be able to pick up their signals and interfere or disable them," James told us.

We listened intently to everything they told us, and we learned more fighting techniques and what to do in different fighting situations—how to attack someone with a ranged weapon or a melee weapon, how to attack from a higher or lower level, and even how to fight hand-to-hand in case we lost our weapons.

Learning how to disarm someone was extremely hard; you had to do it just right. If you weren't quick enough, you'd die. If you grabbed the wrong part of the weapon or the wrong part of the arm holding it, you'd die. It was a scary process.

Once most of us had gotten the hang of something, we'd move on to the next skill. I could tell James and Theo were in a hurry to get us ready for the mission. We were losing more time every day. But we were quick learners. It was in our DNA, Theo had told us. Whenever he talked about it, I'd get confused. I like to know stuff. I don't care why or how something happens; I just want to know *what* happens.

One day, as we were fighting, Theo and James examined our skills very closely. "Again," they would say. We'd resume fighting though we were panting from exhaustion. They would line us up in the ranges, have us shoot or throw for what seemed like forever, and keep pushing us. We were determined in spite of the difficulty. We didn't discuss anything or learn any new skills; we just fought, and for four hours instead of three.

At one point, I had to take a break to catch my breath. "Please tell me training's over."

"It is," James said. "Go sit with your friends."

None of us said anything. We were worn out. We watched Theo and James whispering to each other. They nodded. They turned to us.

"We have watched you, trained you, and taught you. We have decided you are ready for your mission."

29

"You will start your journey tomorrow. We will help you pack tonight," Theo said, but I wasn't sure if anyone was listening. We were awestruck. Time to save the world.

Except for the protesting groans of the elevator, the ride to the surface was silent. When we came out, it was early in the afternoon. We had started training very early that day.

"Into the shop everyone," Theo said.

Theo walked up to the two customers there and told the shop was closing for maintenance for the rest of the day.

Once they left, he locked the door and put the "Closed" sign up. He headed to the windowless back of the shop. "You need to pack only what you'll need, absolutely no more. Only one knapsack each." He reached into a storage closet for some knapsacks that he distributed to us. "Water, money, clothes, and any weapons or tools you need to bring. Always carry your SCDs, and bring an extra battery. You'll want backup flashlights too. You'll be carrying some compact sleeping bags."

I opened my bag and saw a sleeping bag, SCD, battery, and flashlight.

"We have already packed some things for you," Theo said, "but you will do the rest. Take a water bottle to refill, but don't bring more than a few snacks. Buy what food you need; don't carry it. You will need to move quickly. You do not need extra weight to slow you down particularly if you're running for your lives."

My grandfather sounded like a general talking to troops before battle. It was appropriate.

"Hide your weapons. You will be in public, running around in plain sight. You could cause panic if people saw your weapons. Store them in your bag or pocket if possible. If not, we will make adjustments. And never show anyone the power of the amulets. We are counting on you to handle this mission calmly," Theo told us.

"We will send you the coordinates of the amulets' locations," James said. "You will get help on the way from many people in our organization. Once you have collected all the amulets, we will track down Nightshade and send you to him unless he comes first. He may send minions or monsters after you, but try not to fight in front of the public. We have a deadline, the eclipse. We have to retrieve all the amulets and destroy Nightshade before that."

We were anxious, but we felt ready, prepared. We had worked so hard at developing our skills that going on a life-or-death mission seemed normal. I wondered if our quest would change us. The thought of one of us dying terrified me. But we were all tough, all resolved. I knew we would pull through together. Livia smiled at me, not a super happy one, just a contented one. I wondered what was going on in her head.

"Get their weapons, please," Theo asked James, who unlocked a door and went in.

"Where does that lead to?" I asked.

"A staircase down to the cellar. We use it only when no one is in the shop," Theo said.

James returned with our weapons and distributed them.

"Jayce, I forgot to show you something," James said as he handed me my spear. "Hit the bottom of it on the floor."

I let the spear hit the floor with a thud, and it shrank to the size of a stick less than a foot long. "That's how you will carry it around." James smiled, pleased at his creation. "To make it a spear again, flick your wrist like Luna does with her crystal." I tried it a few times and was fascinated by its transformations, which reminded me of Pinocchio's nose.

Livia's mace had a cool feature that allowed the chain and spikes to retract when she pushed two buttons simultaneously. Emmett's bow would morph into a strap for his bag when he placed it around his shoulders, while his quiver was small enough to fit in his bag. Zack's, Terri's, and Luna's weapons were small enough to fit in their pockets or bags.

Once we got settled, James and Theo gave us $500 each. I whistled. "This is a *lot* of money. Are you sure we should take it all?"

Theo laughed. "Yes you should. You will need it. Besides, with all the technology we have, I'm pretty sure we can make more money."

James retrieved filtered water bottles and long-lasting snacks from the closet.

"You guys sure are prepared for us to go on this mission," Zack said.

James nodded. "We've been waiting for this day a long time. Now that it has arrived, I'm glad we spent so much time prepping you for it."

"You are ready," Theo said with a smile. "Put your knapsacks in your rooms. You have the afternoon free. But do not get too tired. Your mission starts tomorrow."

We made plans to meet at the pole with the signs after we stored our bags in our rooms. As Terri and I went to the pole, I saw Calypso and smiled. Terri reached her hand up, and Calypso jumped on it. My sister giggled at the feel of the bird's tiny claws on her finger.

"Is that the famous red bird you keep telling us about?" Zack asked as he and Emmett walked closer. Terri held her up.

"Her name is Calypso, but we still don't know where she came from," I said.

She flew to Emmett and perched on his shoulder. He laughed nervously. "I've never been a roost for a bird before." He seemed cautious about it but intrigued as well.

I heard Luna chuckle and come up behind him. She held up a finger, which Calypso flew to. "Such a friendly bird," she said as she and the bird eyed each other.

Livia joined us shortly. "Jayce, you want to work on that tree house?" She smiled.

The last time I was there, Nightshade had attacked me. We hadn't worked on it much since.

"I'd love to, but ..." I looked to our other friends for their opinions.

Zack smiled. "Go ahead. We don't mind. Meet you guys for dinner?"

"Of course."

Livia and I held hands and walked to the trail. She sighed.

"What's wrong?" I squeezed her hand.

"Nothing. It's just ... strange to be doing something as normal as this. Just holding hands, walking down a trail. I didn't know that the day you came here would be the last normal day of my life."

"It's nice, though. I'm glad we have some free time before our mission to be regular people one last time before our lives change."

"Yeah, I guess so." She squeezed my hand back.

We reached the tree house. She clung tightly to me as I flew to the top. Most of the wood was already up there from our last visit, so we started to build. It didn't take long to get the base as well as some support beams done. We didn't talk much, but we enjoyed each other's company.

After a while, she asked softly, "Do you think *we* will change on the mission?"

I turned from my hammering to her. She seemed sad. No, not sad. Maybe upset. "I don't think we will, not at all."

"I'm ... I'm worried. About us. About you." Her eyes had a soft, sad look.

"We'll be okay. I promise never to let you go no matter what happens." I held her close. I closed my eyes. We listened to the calm rustle of the leaves. I pulled back, grasped her shoulders, and looked at her. "I won't let anything happen to you."

Livia smiled. She had never looked more beautiful. I kissed her.

We got back to work. We added railings and a ladder. I made a small table and chairs with our scrap wood. We worked quickly and efficiently and finished up around dinnertime.

I exhaled. "We're done."

"It was a fun project."

"Definitely."

We smiled and giggled. We descended the ladder.

"I want to see the bunker one last time," I said.

Livia took me down to the big oak tree with the loose roots. She tore them out, and we walked through the tunnel. The bunker was the same as I had remembered—tables and chairs, pictures and boards, the foldable cot I slept on when I was injured.

Livia touched the pictures thumbtacked to the board. "All of that research, hacking into the security cameras, and coming up with theories ..." She looked at each one curiously. "I knew something was up, but I didn't know it was all *true*. And to think there was even more ..." Her voice changed to a whisper. "It's fascinating to see how much can change in just a few weeks."

I tried to figure out what she was thinking, but she was a real puzzle.

She reached into a bag and pulled out two small boxes. "We'll need these on the mission."

"What's in them?"

"Skullcap pills. It's an herb that decreases your heart rate. When I heard about our mission, I got anxious and started to prepare, including making these. I did research to make sure they weren't lethal, and I found some in the woods. They don't stop your heart completely, but if you're lucky, you might be able to trick someone into thinking you were dead. It's only for emergencies though. You must make sure to take only one, otherwise you could have some weird side effects."

The little boxes made me nervous. Inside were pills that no one had tried, and no one knew for sure what would happen. She gave one box to me, which I put it in my pocket, and Livia put the other into her backpack. I swore to myself I'd use a pill in only a life-or-death situation.

"Let's go to dinner," I blurted out. The skullcap herb made me nervous. I wanted to forget about it.

We met the others at the restaurant. Livia didn't say anything about the skullcap pills. I had hoped she wouldn't. We ordered a large pizza, just like our first night together as friends, while Livia had just a salad. I still couldn't figure out why she didn't like pizza. It was better than the first time—a perfect combo of cheese, pepperoni, and perfectly cooked crust. Nobody talked as we ate slice after slice. Nobody said no to ordering another either.

In the middle of our feast, I looked around at my friends' happy faces. *This is our last meal on the island. Tomorrow, everything changes.* But my hunger got the better of me. I kept eating and soon forgot the thought. We ordered ice cream and talked not about our mission but about our good times on the island.

"Remember when I tackled Zack at the campfire?" Emmett asked. "That was fun."

Zack laughed. "I totally won that fight. I pinned you down easily."

"Not *that* easily. I got away."

I smiled as the two debated the matter. Zack was finally able to convince Emmett he had won, and everyone laughed.

We quieted down. Terri said, "I'm gonna miss this. Fun dinners, campfires, joking around with you all."

"Yeah, you guys are pretty awesome though you boys get too crazy sometimes," Livia said with a chuckle.

"Hey," Zack said, "that's why we're here. Right?"

Emmett and I agreed.

We toasted each other. Sadly, our dinner came to an end. We said goodnight. Terri and I broke off from the group one last time to go to the shop as they walked to the hotel.

Theo was waiting at the door. "Rest. Tomorrow will be exhausting. Make sure everything is packed before you go to sleep." We nodded and marched up to our room.

Terri listlessly threw herself onto the bed. "I'm tired," she said with a moan.

"I see that," I said as I sorted through my knapsack. I pulled out the little box from my pocket. In it were two light-blue pills. I shoved it into my bag.

I eventually crawled into my bed but tossed and turned, afraid of what might happen on our mission. I couldn't get to sleep. I dressed and snuck downstairs and out.

It was cool outside. Lights on the path illuminated the way. I walked a bit to clear my head of the overwhelming details of the mission. I looked up. I saw someone hunched over on a bench staring at the ground. I walked closer. "Luna?"

She didn't move. I sat next to her. "Why are you out?"
I saw tears on her cheeks. She stared straight ahead.
"Luna, what's wrong?"
"I can't do this."
"What do you mean?"
She looked at me. "I can't go on this mission. I'm too unstable. I'll just mess things up. I can't control myself."
"You won't cause any problems on the mission."
"I will, and you know that, Jayce. Nightshade will use me as a tool or a minion. I'll drag you guys down."
"Luna, look at me. You're not going to mess anything up, okay? I know you can control it."
She shook her head. "I've tried. There's no way."
"I want you to close your eyes and imagine that ball of anger and darkness controlling you." She closed her eyes. "I want you to imagine yourself grabbing that ball of darkness and crushing it. Imagine it crumbling under your power. You're in charge. You won't let it control you. Just breathe."
I put a hand on her shoulder, and my amulet grew warm. I tried to feel calm and transfer the feeling to her, but I didn't think it was working. But after a few moments, I felt her relax a little.
"I'll try," she said.
That was all I needed to hear. "Go. Sleep. We all need rest."
She walked toward the hotel. When she entered it, I headed to my room.
I tiptoed up the stairs and winced whenever the floors creaked. Knowing I had helped Luna, I was finally able to sleep.

30

I woke up to the sound of my grandfather cheer-fully yelling, "Today's the day! Meet me in the shop in twenty minutes." He slipped out the door.

I got dressed in the most comfortable shorts and T-shirt I could find and packed some last-minute things, including pens and my journal. I was ready.

"All set, Terri?"

"Almost." She was still trying to stuff some things into her bag.

We headed down and saw our friends. Everyone sat in the same spot in the shop as the previous day.

James spoke. "We have prepared and trained you as best we could. It's time for you to go. The first place you'll go to will have people who will help you, but you'll be mostly on your own. We bid you good luck. Always try your hardest. Not all the amulets will be easy to get to, so always be careful and alert."

We went over a checklist to make sure we had every-thing. We tested our SCDs. We were ready. Theo said, "Jayce, Terri, I need your help. Follow me."

He led us up the stairs and to his room. He reached

for the doorknob. I would finally get to see what was in his room and why we had been forbidden to enter it. He opened the door. I saw nothing out of the ordinary for a bedroom. Until he pressed a button under a desk. A panel in a wall slid open, revealing a big metal box with two keys and a giant lever. "Jayce, Terri, you two turn the keys at the same time when I say three." He reached for the lever.

"Is this what we're going to use for moving to our first location?" I asked. Theo nodded.

"One … two … three!" Terri and I turned the keys. Theo pulled the switch. We heard loud humming and machinery clicking and moving.

"What's happening?" Terri asked as the floor vibrated.

Theo said nothing. He led us out and down the stairs.

James and Theo were calm as the rest of us were freaking out.

"What's going on?" Livia asked me.

"I don't know! We turned some keys in locks, Theo pulled a switch, and then the shaking started!"

The sounds finally stopped.

"What was that?" Zack asked.

"We activated it," Theo simply said. I hated it when he was so vague about what he was talking about.

"Activated *what*?" Zack was insistent.

James opened the door to the cellar. We descended to the dusty room. "Into the elevator, please."

Once everyone was squeezed in, the elevator doors shut. I saw the third button glowing. Theo pressed it, and we lurched down, past the training room, deep into the ground. The elevator doors opened to a dark room. We walked off the elevator and into not that big a space.

"Lights, please," I requested impatiently.

Someone flicked a switch. A soft hum. Blindingly bright lights. The room was empty except for a big control panel and a metal frame about twice my height but only a few people wide. Countless wires led from it to the control panel, but the inside of the frame was empty.

And then it hit me. *A portal? No way!*

It took a moment for my friends to get it, but they figured it out as well.

James and Theo were working the control panel. I heard beeps and switches being flipped as well as buttons being clicked.

"Theo, the aegris please."

Theo handed it to him.

I leaned over to see what was going on and saw a big circle in the middle of the control panel with a few buttons and codes written on it, but in the middle was a hole, a hole the exact shape of the aegris.

James placed the ring into the slot and turned the whole thing. Everything started humming louder and louder until it sounded like it was shrieking. I covered my ears.

A pop. A flash of light. I blinked a few times and turned to the portal. It was a crazy blue color. It looked like an illusion. It was swirling and stretching, changing in a thousand different ways. It almost hurt to even look at it. The portal made a mystifying sound, something I couldn't describe. It warped and hummed like a distorted song.

"This is how you will arrive at your first location," James said.

Zack walked forward, but Theo stopped him. "Jayce and Terri go first."

My sister and I stepped forward. We gave each other worried looks. "Ready?" I asked her.

"If you are."

I looked at Theo and James. "Thanks for everything." They nodded.

I smiled at Terri. She smiled back.

We jumped into the portal.

The feeling of being transported by portal was ... well, it's hard to explain. I felt like I had turned into clay and someone was squishing and molding me into different shapes. I felt like pudding flopping around. I couldn't see anything other than the swirling, blue light. I wondered if Terri was having the same feeling.

In a few minutes, I felt myself solidifying. I fell out of the portal and landed with a thud on the ground. I heard Terri land next to me. I lifted my head and saw two men. They weren't Theo and James.

"Welcome. We've been expecting you," an unfamiliar voice said.

I didn't recognize the one who had spoken. But the other man came closer. I knew who he was. It was the craziest moment in all my fifteen years. I'd never thought it would come, but here it was. I used to think many things were impossible, but that day told me nothing was. It really sunk in that my life was about to get very interesting.

"Welcome, Jayce and Terri. It's time for the start of your mission."

The man was our father.

CPSIA information can be obtained
at www.ICGtesting.com
Printed in the USA
LVOW12*1422261017
553881LV00007B/48/P

9 781480 831452